D0976412

THE GIFT OF LOVE

When young Toby's mother, Jane, dies, his Aunt Shona and her family rally round to look after him. Shona helps to run Jane's Florist, selling the roses from her father's nursery. Then another cloud looms on the horizon. Mrs Tynedale, the elderly owner of the land on which the nursery stands, is considering selling up. Her grandson, Mallory, has come to help her make the right decision. Shona soon learns that mixing business with pleasure can lead to heartbreak.

THE GIFT OF LOVE

THE GIFT OF LOVE

Complete and Unabridged

LINFORD
Leicester

First published in Great Britain in 2009

First Linford Edition
published 2010

British Library CIP Data

Long, Jean M.
  The gift of love. - -
  (Linford romance library)
  1. Florists- -Fiction.
  2. Nursery growers- -Fiction.
  3. Love stories. 4. Large type books.
  I. Title II. Series
  823.9'14–dc22

  ISBN 978–1–44480–340–2

Published by
F. A. Thorpe (Publishing)
Anstey, Leicestershire

Set by Words & Graphics Ltd.
Anstey, Leicestershire
Printed and bound in Great Britain by
T. J. International Ltd., Padstow, Cornwall

This book is printed on acid-free paper

A Complicated Family Arrangement

Shona put the finishing touches to the basket of flowers and examined her handiwork critically. No, it still wasn't quite right. Catching sight of the clock, she frowned. Toby should have been back from Friday Club by now.

From the shop window she could see right across Woodhurst Green but there was no sign of her young nephew. Just as she reached for the phone a silver grey Mercedes came into view and swished to a halt nearby. To her relief, Toby came hurtling out and raced along the pathway to Jane's Florist. A moment later the door burst open.

'Sorry, Auntie Shona! Peter hurt his knee in P.E. and his mum took him to casualty so Mr Tynedale gave me a lift instead,' he informed her breathlessly.

1

'Poor Peter! You really ought to have rung me, Toby. I'd have collected you . . . anyway, who on earth is Mr Tynedale?'

'I am, who's asking?' The man who had followed Toby into the shop was tall and of medium build with a mop of chestnut hair. He leant over the shop counter, grey eyes surveying her with a hint of amusement.

'I'm Toby's aunt,' she told him, her hazel eyes meeting his gaze coolly. 'Thanks for giving him a lift. Have you left your son in the car?'

'My son?' His eyebrows shot up.

Toby turned pink and said quickly, 'Mr Tynedale takes Friday Club with Mrs Jennings.'

Before Shona could reply Mr Tynedale smiled and stretched out a hand.

'Let's begin again, shall we? Mallory Tynedale.'

'Shona Sutton.' As she took his hand, she was aware of a slight tingling sensation in her fingers and caught her breath. She supposed her young assistant, Kylie, would probably have described the man

2

standing in front of her as being, 'Dishy.' Light suddenly dawned on her.

'Are you, by any chance, Mrs Tynedale's grandson?'

He inclined his head. 'That's me! Actually, I'm killing two birds with one stone, Miss Sutton. I rang up and ordered a basket of flowers this morning, so I'll collect it, if it's ready.'

Shona immediately became business-like. 'Of course, I'm just finishing the arrangement now. Perhaps you'd like a coffee whilst you're waiting? Toby switch the kettle on, please.'

Mallory Tynedale perched on the edge of a stool and watched as Shona bent over the flower arrangement, thinking what a pretty girl she was. She had an abundance of dark hair framing a heart-shaped face, large, expressive eyes and a gorgeous figure.

'I know what's missing,' she told him, and selecting three apricot roses from a vase, held them up for his approval. 'How about these?'

'Wonderful! My grandmother adores

roses. Do you buy them in from the nursery near us?'

Shona was surprised by his question. Surely he knew her family ran both businesses?

'Well, of course, we . . . ' She trailed off as Toby careered into the shop again.

'Kettle's boiled,' he announced. 'Can I go and see Sammi?'

'Just for ten minutes and then I want you back here pronto — understood?'

He grinned and saluted cheekily before dashing off to find his friend, Samantha Hardy, whose parents managed the newsagent's across the green.

As Shona returned with the coffee, Mallory Tynedale said, 'You know there's something puzzling me here. I thought Mollie Browne, at the rose nursery, was Toby's grandmother.'

She handed him a mug of coffee and indicated the sugar bowl. 'Yes, she is. Why?'

'Toby told me this used to be his mother's shop, but now it's his grandmother's.'

'That's right.' Shona confirmed. 'But

he actually means my mother, who's his other grandmother. It's a bit complicated. Would you like me to draw you a family tree?'

He was startled by her sharp tone. 'I'm sorry if you think I'm intruding. I was just trying to get my head round it, that's all.'

Shona was immediately contrite. 'I'm afraid we've had quite a traumatic time recently and there've been quite a few changes in our lives. Anyway, in a nutshell, Mollie Browne and my father run the rose nursery jointly. Mollie's son, Rob, is Toby's father, but you obviously know that already. My sister, Jane, was Rob's wife and she and my mother ran the shop together, but she died last year.'

Shona's eyes clouded as she thought of Toby's mother who had been such a warm, vibrant person. Life could be cruel she reflected, but tragedies brought out the best in people.

Mallory Tynedale looked sympathetic. 'Yes, I'm so sorry. I heard about the skiing accident. It must have been devastating for you all.'

'We're still trying to come to terms with it, but life has to go on. My mother loves floristry and so she's taken over Jane's business. As I've already explained, she's Toby's other grand-mother, most people have at least two, don't they?'

He laughed. 'And you're helping out today?'

'Not just today. I've recently moved here so I can help look after Toby whilst his father's away and lend a hand with the two businesses.'

A few months after Jane had died, Rob had suddenly announced that he'd got an engineering contract overseas and so her family had rallied round, creating a new and caring home for Toby as he didn't feel any further disruption should feature in young Toby's life.

Mallory Tynedale looked thoughtful. 'Right. I hadn't actually taken on board, until now, that both the rose nursery and the florist came under the same umbrella.'

Shona nodded. She trimmed the roses and placed them carefully into the basket. 'There, what d'you think?' she asked.

'Perfect,' he told her. 'It's my grandmother's birthday so I'm taking her out for a meal tonight and these are just an additional present.'

On an impulse, Shona scooped a small posy of bright summer flowers from a bucket of water and wrapped it expertly.

'Please take her this and wish her a very happy birthday from us all.'

She liked Mrs Tynedale who owned the land that the rose nursery stood on, together with some shares in the business.

'That's very kind of you, Miss, er, Sutton — a nice gesture. Thanks for the coffee too.'

'You're welcome and thank you again for bringing Toby back from school. I'd better go and round him up.'

7

Mallory picked up the flowers. 'He's a very well adjusted lad considering all that he's been through,' he commented.

'Yes, children adapt to new situations remarkably quickly, providing they have a secure and stable environment. We were a bit worried when his father went abroad and Toby had to come and live with my parents . . . ' Shona trailed off, wondering why she was finding it so easy to talk to this stranger. Just recently she'd spent so long trying to support the rest of the family through this difficult time that she'd bottled up her own emotions.

'Anyway, I must close up,' she told Mallory Tynedale somewhat abruptly.

He took the hint and she watched as he walked towards his car, carefully carrying the basket of flowers in one hand and the posy in the other. He paused to speak to Toby who was holding a comic and she wondered how Mrs Tynedale's grandson came to be involved with Toby's school. He seemed pleasant enough and he was so good

8

looking. Hold on, she told herself sternly. You're practically engaged to Adrian. Just because he's in Africa that's no excuse to be disloyal.

★ ★ ★

As they drove the short distance to his grandparents' bungalow, Toby immersed himself in his comic.

'Tell me, Toby, how come Mr Tynedale helps out at Friday Club? Is he one of your teachers?' Shona asked curiously.

'Nope, but he's a brilliant artist and that's what some of us are doing this term. He's got a studio in Mrs Tynedale's garden. She's his grand-mother, did you know?'

'Well yes, I sort of guessed and, anyway, he bought the flowers for her.'

'He's a bit old to have a grand-mother, don't you think? Although Mrs Tynedale is really ancient.'

'Don't let either of your grans hear you saying that,' she warned him laughingly. 'Anyway, I had a grand-mother until four years ago, so I was twenty-six when she died. She was your great-grandma — surely you remember?'

'Of course, but I was only little then. She used to give me sweets and pocket money.'

Shona turned into a leafy lane. 'So how long has Mr Tynedale been helping with your Friday Club?'

Toby screwed up his face in concentration. 'Not sure, he was around for the school play at Easter. He's a friend of Mrs Jennings. We think she's divorced. That's what Sammi's mum said.'

'Did she indeed? Well, perhaps you shouldn't listen to gossip.'

Toby turned to look out of the window and shortly afterwards, Shona pulled into the driveway of her parents' bungalow, realising that the thought of Mallory Tynedale and Toby's elegant headmistress, Elaine Jennings, as an item, struck a discordant note. She shook her head as if to free herself of the thought.

As they entered the kitchen, Edward Sutton looked up with a smile, blue eyes twinkling. 'Hello, you two, how've your days been?'

They told him briefly and then Toby rushed off to change out of his school clothes.

'So how've things been at the nursery?' Shona wanted to know, thinking how weary her father looked. 'Did you manage OK with one short?'

'But, of course, Mollie Browne and your mother will be proud of me. Well, let's hope their day at Hampton Court has been as good as ours. They certainly deserved a treat.'

Shona washed her hands at the kitchen sink. 'I've just met Mrs Tynedale's grandson. Did you know he was helping out with Toby's Friday Club, Dad?'

'Yes, Toby did mention it. I gather Mallory's come to keep his grand-mother company for a few months.

11

Since her husband died at the beginning of the year she's found it difficult to adjust to being in that large place on her own. She is rather housebound these days — bad arthritis. Apparently Mallory wants to have a look round the rose nursery sometime soon. Mollie thinks he'll be sizing us up!'

'Mollie's got a suspicious mind!' Shona laughed. 'Toby says Mr Tynedale's friendly with Mrs Jennings,' she added casually.

Her father put down his newspaper. 'Well, I think they probably go back a long way. I gather from Mollie they've been friends for years . . . ' He trailed off as Toby came rushing back into the room.

'What's for tea? I'm starving!'

His grandfather surveyed him fondly and ruffled his fair hair.

'Yes, it looks as if you are. Well, it just won't do, Shona! What is for tea?'

'Well, as you boys have been so good, for a treat we're allowed fish and chips!'

'Great! But who's going to get them?' Toby asked, impatiently shifting from one foot to the other.

His grandfather sighed, 'Looks as if it'd better be me, just as I was about to watch the news. Coming with me, lad?'

Shona grinned as she watched the two of them marching off down the path together. Her father and Toby were great pals, which was just as well seeing as her nephew's own father had deserted him, if only on a temporary basis.

To give him his due, Rob had attempted to make a go of things when Jane had died, but he'd found it increasingly difficult to cope with the situation. And then, just before Easter, he'd taken up the offer of the job abroad, saying he needed some space to sort himself out.

Toby's grandparents had stepped in to look after the boy. Running both the rose nursery and Jane's Florist kept them fully occupied, however, and they had found it increasingly difficult to manage. In the end, Shona had decided that the only solution would be to leave her own job in London and come and help out in Woodhurst so that they could all have a bit more time to spend with Toby.

After putting the plates to warm, Shona set to and prepared a side salad. Her mother had left a trifle in the fridge for dessert.

'Not more rabbit food!' her father said jokingly, surveying the table as they sat down for their supper a short while later. 'So what did you do in Friday Club, Toby?'

Toby reached for the ketchup. 'Batik — we finished it off from last time.'

'Great! So where is it then?' asked Shona.

'I gave it to Mr Tynedale for his grandmother, it's her birthday,' he told his grandfather.

'Well that was a nice thing to do,' Edward Sutton said, winking at Shona.

'I like Mrs Tynedale,' Toby said. 'She's got a little dog called Juniper.'

'Dog!' Shona sprang to her feet.

'Dad, did you remember to feed Mollie's dog?'

'Of course I did. What do you take me for? And Josh took her for a walk, so relax. Toby tells me Mallory Tynedale gave him a lift back from school today.'

'Yes, he came into the shop.' She filled him in and then Toby piped up.

'Sammi's mum's taking her to the seaside, not this Sunday but the next one. She says I can come too, if I want — so can I? You're always busy.'

His grandfather looked at him sharply. 'Toby haven't you forgotten something?'

Toby looked puzzled. 'What?'

'Grandma Browne's taking you to see her sister next Sunday, isn't she?'

He looked crestfallen and muttered something under his breath.

'Come on, Toby, you like Auntie Sylvia, and your dad's cousin, Julie, will be there with her children. You get on well with Tom and Lucy, don't you?' Shona put in quickly, attempting to avert a scene.

'I suppose so, but does it have to be next Sunday? I haven't been to the seaside for yonks because everyone's always working.'

'Sorry, old chap,' Mr Sutton said. 'It's all arranged now. It's a pity you can't go with Sammi, but these things happen. Now don't look like that! Finish your supper.'

Toby pushed his plate away. 'I'm not hungry any more. I wish Dad was here, he'd let me go.'

'I doubt it,' Shona told him. 'It's bad manners to accept an invitation and then back out because you've got a better offer. I take it you don't want any pudding?'

Toby brightened. 'What is it?'

'Trifle and ice cream,' Shona said matter-of-factly.

Toby thought for a moment and then pulled his unfinished tea towards him and polished it off rapidly.

Shona felt a surge of sympathy for the boy, but he had to learn that he couldn't have things all his own way.

Her sister would never have allowed it and Shona strongly suspected that Rob had given into him when she had died, as if to compensate, which made it difficult for them now.

Mollie Browne and Kathleen Sutton arrived back at eight o'clock, full of their day out at the Hampton Court Palace Flower Show. It was good they got on so well, especially as Mollie's husband had died barely a year before Jane. The two women had been a great support to each other. The rose nursery was a thriving concern nowadays, but when George Browne died, it began to go downhill and Mollie Browne had talked of selling up.

The following morning, Shona was up at the crack of dawn to be there for the deliveries at Jane's Florist. Saturday was one of their busiest times. Toby was going to stay with his grandfather in the morning and then Shona had arranged to take him and Sammi to the cinema in the afternoon. Kathleen Sutton had had a little word with Sammi's mother on the phone, explaining why Toby couldn't accompany them to the seaside the following Sunday.

For once Kylie was in bright and early to help Shona in the shop, and together they sorted out the delivery and were all ready to open up by nine o'clock.

'You look as if you had a great time last night,' Shona commented.

Kylie grinned and shook back her long, dark hair. 'Certainly did! Scott and I went to that new nightclub in town. You should try it some time.'

Shona tried to remember when she had last been to a club. And then she did remember and wished she hadn't. It had been on the occasion when Adrian had told her he was going to Africa to do his V.S.O.

There was a steady stream of customers during the course of the morning. Mrs Sutton arrived at about ten-thirty, looking as neat as ever with not a hair out of place.

'Mum, I told you we could manage,' Shona protested.

19

Mrs Sutton smiled at her daughter, popped on her overall and picked up the order book. 'Oh, you know me, never happy unless I'm busy. Anyway, I had a lovely day out yesterday with Mollie and we picked up quite a few ideas. Who knows perhaps we'll exhibit one day!'

'Well, you already do, locally. How about I make us all some coffee before I take these buttonholes over to the church for the wedding?'

The rest of the morning flew past and, after a hasty lunch, Shona collected Toby and Sammi and they set off to the cinema for the latest Harry Potter film. It was a full house, crowded with excited children and so Shona was glad they'd got there early.

'There's Mr Tynedale!' Sammi said, as they made their way out at the end of the film.

Following the child's gaze, Shona found herself looking directly at him. He was holding a small girl by the hand and accompanied by an attractive blonde woman.

Shona swallowed, wondering who his companions were. For a brief moment, their eyes met and then, in the crush, they went their separate ways.

'I'm sorry what did you say, Toby?'

'I said I wonder if that's his girlfriend.'

Sammi stared at him, blue eyes wide. 'But she can't be. What about Mrs Jennings? You don't think he's two-timing her, do you?'

Shona said, 'Whatever makes you say that, Sammi?'

'That's what happened to Toyah who works in our shop. I heard her tell my mum she dumped her boyfriend because he two-timed her!'

'Right — well, let's not even go there.' Shona said briskly. 'Now, who's for an ice cream? I need a coffee before I go home.'

They went into a café in the cinema complex and it wasn't until the waiter had taken their order that Toby said, 'Look, they're over there in the corner!'

'Who?' demanded Sammi.

Glancing across the restaurant, Shona saw the elegant, blonde woman talking animatedly with Mallory Tynedale over cups of coffee, whilst the little girl was ploughing her way through a huge ice cream.

'That looks serious,' Toby said.

'Don't you dare let them catch you staring at them,' Shona whispered.

Fortunately, just then, their ice creams arrived followed by her cappuccino and the children were too occupied to continue their surveillance. Shona wondered if Mallory Tynedale was a Casanova or if it was just idle speculation that he was dating Mrs Jennings. A sudden thought struck her, perhaps the child was his and the woman his wife. Maybe they were separated or divorced. She pulled herself together sharply as Toby waved a hand in front of her eyes.

'Come back, Auntie Shona! Can we go to that shop in the centre before we go home?'

She consulted her watch. 'There really isn't time, Toby. It'll be closed by half past five. If your pocket money's burning a hole in your pocket, I'll see if I can fit it in after school one day.'

At that moment, Mallory Tynedale and party walked practically past their table and, noticing them, Mallory raised his hand in recognition and gave them a smile.

* * *

Shona accompanied her mother, Mollie Browne and Toby to church the following morning. On the opposite side of the aisle, she caught sight of Mrs Tynedale and Mallory.

After the service everyone went into the church hall for coffee. When Shona joined the queue she found herself standing behind Mallory Tynedale.

'Hi,' he said in a friendly manner. 'This is a bit of a bun fight, isn't it?'

'It's the only time some people have to socialise,' she told him.

'I wasn't criticising — just observing,' he replied, a twinkle in his eyes. 'Did you enjoy the Harry Potter film yesterday?'

'Not as much as the children did. How about you?'

'Oh, I'm just a big kid myself, so I was completely enraptured the entire time.'

They reached the hatch and collected their refreshments. When she returned to their table, it was to see Toby pulling up a chair for Mrs Tynedale. She was so elegant, Shona thought, immaculately dressed with beautifully coiffeured silver hair.

'I'm glad I've seen you,' the elderly lady told them, settling herself more comfortably on the rather hard chair. 'I wanted to thank you all for the lovely flowers. Such a kind gesture and your picture was quite something, Toby. Now, I'd like you to come to tea this afternoon, shall we say around four o'clock?'

It sounded like a royal command,

Shona reflected.

'It's very kind of you, Mrs Tynedale, but I'm afraid we've got a prior engagement,' Mollie told her apologetically. 'At least Kathleen and myself have. Joyce Wallis from W.I. is expecting us to call on her after the nursery closes. She wants us to meet her cousin who's staying with her.'

Mrs Tynedale looked disappointed and Kathleen Sutton, who had a warm heart, said quickly, 'But, I'm sure Shona and Toby will be only too pleased to accept your kind invitation.'

Toby opened his mouth to say something, but was quelled by a glance from his grandmother and closed it again. Shona felt obliged to accept the offer graciously, noticing that Mallory was looking rather amused.

After a hectic week, she'd been looking forward to spending a nice, quiet afternoon sunbathing outside her caravan, which was parked in Paddy's Field, adjacent to the nursery.

Veronica Tynedale smiled. 'That's

good, my great grandchildren are staying with me for the weekend and it'll be nice for them to meet Toby.'

Her great-grandchildren! How many were there? Shona had a flashback to the cinema the previous day. So where were the blonde woman and the children this morning?

'They've gone riding this morning,' Mrs Tynedale said, as if reading her thoughts.

Shona found herself heartily wishing that she hadn't been coerced into accepting the invitation to tea, and knew it was because she didn't want to watch Mallory playing at happy families!

Toby gave vent to his feelings as they headed home.

'Sammi and I were going for a bike ride this afternoon,' he complained.

'Well, there's been a change of plan,' Kathleen Sutton told him firmly. 'Anyway, I don't remember you mentioning it to me. I thought you liked Mrs Tynedale.'

26

'I do but, well, there are rather a lot of grandmas round here!' and he raced off.

'That young man needs taking in hand,' Mollie Browne said, lips pursed.

Kathleen Sutton sighed. 'There have been a lot of changes for him just lately. It must be very different from his old life.'

Shona felt a bit sorry for her nephew, who was a typical ten-year-old and, naturally missed his father kicking a football around with him at the weekends or taking him swimming.

'Well, not to worry, I'm here now and I'll take him up to Rose Lodge so that you two can go on your visit and Dad can have a bit of quality time with the newspapers,' she told them lightly, wondering what exactly she was letting herself in for that afternoon!

Concerns About The Nursery

After a traditional Sunday lunch, Shona wasn't sure if she could manage any tea. At precisely ten to four, however, she set off with Toby firmly in tow. Despite his protests, she had insisted he dressed in his Sunday best again, rather than his usual jeans and T-shirt. She herself was wearing a pink linen skirt and white top and had swept up her hair in a loose knot.

Shona had been in the grounds of Rose Lodge several times when there had been functions, but never in the house itself and she was curious to see the inside of it. The door was opened by Mallory Tynedale who greeted them with a smile.

'Hello, you two, come along in.'

Crossing a spacious hall, they were

ushered into a large sitting room full of highly polished antique furniture. Mrs Tynedale was sitting in a high-backed chair in one corner and facing her was the attractive fair-haired woman from the cinema. The little girl and a boy about Toby's age, were stroking a King Charles spaniel.

Mrs Tynedale looked up with a smile, and Shona realised that it reminded her of Mallory's. In spite of being in her eighties she was still an attractive woman.

'Well, this is delightful! Forgive me if I don't get up.'

Shona crossed to the old lady's chair and took her hand, noting the surprisingly firm grip.

Toby stood awkwardly by Shona's side, suddenly lost for words, but Mrs Tynedale put him at his ease, nodding in the direction of the children.

'Toby, those two are Felix and Anya. They're my great-grandchildren. This is Toby and Shona who've come to take tea with us.' She turned to the smartly dressed woman sitting beside her. 'And this is my granddaughter, Miranda. Of course you know Mallory already.'

Things suddenly slotted into place as Shona realised Miranda was Mallory's sister — not his wife or even his girlfriend. And the children were evidently his niece and nephew.

The little girl crossed to Shona's side. 'Are you his mummy?' she asked curiously.

There was a silence and then Toby said in a matter-of-fact tone, 'No, she's my Auntie Shona. I don't have a mother any more. She died.'

'How about we put Juniper in the conservatory?' Mallory suggested to the children, to cover an awkward moment. 'And then you can wash your hands and help me fetch in the tea. I just need to sort out the drinks. Coming, Toby?'

Toby followed, leaving the three women.

'I'm afraid Anya is rather direct,' Mrs Tynedale said apologetically.

'She's only seven, Grandmother,'

Miranda replied, rather defensively.

Mrs Tynedale wisely changed the subject. 'My housekeeper has Sunday afternoons off, but she's left everything ready in the kitchen. Of course, I know I shouldn't say it, but no-one could ever replace Mollie Browne. She and her husband used to run the house and garden like clockwork between them.'

'Well, we all have to get used to change,' Miranda said sharply. She turned to Shona. 'My grandmother tells me you work in that florist shop on the green. Don't you find it boring?' Her tone was patronising.

'Far from it. It's a thriving business situated, as it is, just two miles from town,' Shona told her, refusing to be needled. 'Do you work?'

Miranda was studying her perfectly manicured nails. 'Oh yes. I'm a P.A. I do a job-share. Of course, when you have children you have to consider them.'

Shona nodded. 'That's why I've come to Woodhurst, to help look after Toby.'

Shona was relieved when Mallory entered with the tea trolley shortly afterwards, followed by the three children. She hadn't taken to Miranda at all.

It was a delightful, old-fashioned tea. Sandwiches, scones with jam and cream and individual trifles topped with strawberries.

Mallory and his grandmother kept the conversation flowing whilst Miranda said very little. The children chattered amongst themselves seeming to get along happily enough.

'And now for the pièce de résistance!' Mallory said, winking at the children. He dived outside, to return a few moments later with a magnificent birthday cake, alight with candles.

'We decided to save it for today because Mrs Huggins made us a special chocolate cake for yesterday.'

It was well gone five by the time tea was over and Shona was anxious for them not to outstay their welcome, particularly as Miranda had said, rather pointedly, that she and the children would be leaving by six-thirty.

'Can we go outside for a bit, Great Grandma?' Felix asked, just as Shona was deciding they should make a move.

'I'd let your tea settle, if I were you,' Mrs Tynedale advised him. 'Why don't you have a nice game of that Junior Scrabble I bought you?'

Shona saw the look of horror on Toby's face. Spelling wasn't his strong point and recent events had meant that he was a bit behind with his schoolwork.

She set down her cup and saucer. 'Actually, I think we ought to be making a move. It's been lovely, but . . .'

Mallory sprang to his feet. 'How about we all walk back together? Juniper could do with a walk and Miranda has the children's things to pack up.'

'Six-thirty sharp,' Miranda said. 'Now, if you'll excuse me. There are one or two things I must see to.' She collected up the tea things briskly, mumbled a goodbye and wheeled out the tea trolley with the children and Mallory in her wake.

For a few moments, Shona found herself alone with Mrs Tynedale.

The older woman sighed. 'Miranda is so like her mother, it isn't true, whereas Mallory . . . ' Her features softened. 'Mallory is like his father and my dear late husband, Archie. My son, Thomas, died some years back and I still miss him, particularly on occasions like today. He would have been the life and soul of the party.'

Shona stood there awkwardly, wondering what to say and then, carefully choosing her words she remarked, 'I'm sure the loss of a child, however old, must be devastating to any mother.'

Mrs Tynedale's eyes were full of sadness and Shona's heart went out to her.

'Of course, your poor mother would understand because of Jane. Thomas was so bright, such a terrible loss. It turned out he had a heart defect. Unfortunately, my daughter-in-law and I don't get on too well and, nowadays, I hardly ever see her. It's no secret — Mollie Browne will tell you, if I don't.'

'It happens,' Shona said gently. 'Anyway, I've enjoyed your tea-party and I'm sure Toby has too. Thank you so much for inviting us.'

'I hope you'll come again before long and bring young Toby. Actually, there was a little matter I wanted to ask you about, my dear, although I hardly like to mention it . . . '

She paused and Shona wondered whatever she was about to say. She smiled at her encouragingly and Mrs

Tynedale continued, 'Since my husband died, earlier this year, I'm afraid I've rather lost interest in the garden, but Mallory tells me the roses need some attention. Harry, who does the grounds for me, is really getting a bit old for the job and, anyway, he prefers to potter in the greenhouses mostly, nowadays. Anyway, I was wondering . . . ' she hesitated.

'You'd like my father or Mollie Browne to take a look?' Shona prompted.

Mrs Tynedale looked a bit awkward. 'I would be grateful if you could have a word with them. I realise how busy they both are, particularly now that you're all lending a hand to look after young Toby. George Browne and my husband got on like a house on fire. At one time he worked here full-time, as a gardener, you know.'

Shona nodded. 'And then the Brownes branched out and opened the rose nursery.'

'Yes, with our blessing. We thought it was a brilliant idea, but, of course, it meant that George couldn't spend so much time over here, but one way and another we all managed.'

'Well, I'm sure either my father or Mollie will come over,' Shona assured her.

Veronica Tynedale looked relieved. 'You see, I love the roses, but I can't do too much in the garden nowadays. I confess they've been a bit neglected during these past months, but now Mallory's here things are gradually getting back to normal. He's such a blessing to me. He's going to sort everything out.'

★ ★ ★

During the short walk to the nursery, the children hurried on ahead with Juniper, leaving Shona with Mallory.

'Thanks for coming, Shona. My grandmother so enjoyed it. Unfortunately, my sister finds these visits a bit of a strain, sees them as doing her duty. Anyway, you don't want to know about our family problems.'

On the contrary, Shona found the situation interesting, and was determined to ask Mollie Browne more about the Tynedale family at the earliest opportunity.

'Have you seen Uncle Mal's studio?' Anya asked running back to them.

'Well, no, but I've heard about it,' Shona told her.

'Can we go there now?' the little girl demanded, catching hold of Mallory's hand.

'No time, I'm afraid, poppet. Your mother said you'd be leaving at six-thirty sharp and that's what she meant.'

'Just when we're having fun,' Felix chimed in.

'Well, it's not long till the holidays, so perhaps you can come and stay,' Mallory suggested.

The children brightened. Anya clapped her hands. 'Brilliant! And daddy's taking us to the seaside for a week in August!'

As the children raced ahead once more, Mallory explained. 'Miranda's divorced but her husband still lives fairly nearby. He brought Felix yesterday afternoon whilst the rest of us were at the cinema. Felix didn't want to miss his athletics club and had seen the film already. My grandmother's very fond of Oliver, so it was good that they were able to spend some quality time together. Actually, it's almost a repeat performance of our own childhood. After my father died, we were foisted on my grandparents most holidays too. Not that I'm complaining because we had some wonderful times.'

As they reached the gate leading to the nursery Mallory said, 'If you're interested, you'd be more than welcome to look round the studio when the Friday Club come with Elaine Jennings, Shona, but you'd probably prefer to visit on a separate occasion.'

'Thanks, I'll bear that in mind.' She told him, trying not to seem too keen. 'If you're around, I could always take a look when my father or Mollie come over to see your grandmother's roses.'

Mallory stared at her, frowning slightly. 'I'm sorry? I've afraid you've lost me there.'

She filled him in. 'I thought Mrs Tynedale would have mentioned it to you.'

He shrugged his shoulders. 'Nope, not a word. Mind you, it's a good sign because she hasn't shown much interest in the garden since my grandfather died, and those roses do need some attention. Naturally, I do what I can to help, but there's such a lot of ground here. Besides, I don't want to tread on Harry's toes, but it's getting a bit too much for him nowadays, although he'd be heartbroken if he wasn't allowed to potter about.'

'Well, we'll be tactful,' Shona promised.

They had reached the gate leading to the rose nursery. The children said their goodbyes and Shona and Toby stood waving until the others disappeared from view.

The bungalow was only a short step

from Mrs Browne's house and so, before returning to her caravan, Shona escorted Toby home and passed on Mrs Tynedale's request to her father, who promised to do what he could to help.

The next few days were incredibly busy. Several wreaths for funerals had to be delivered, and then there was an order for a number of table decorations for a big luncheon party at the nearby town hall. There was a box of buttonholes and some posies to make up for a mid-week wedding, and a large floral display for a function in the local golf club.

On Wednesday afternoon, Shona went to help her father in the rose nursery, whilst Mollie Browne took a flower arranging class with a group of young wives at the village hall.

'I've phoned Mrs Tynedale and left a message on her answerphone to say I can take a look at her roses tomorrow afternoon,' her father told her, as he paused in the act of deadheading some of the container roses. 'Of course,

Archie Tynedale was a fount of knowledge when it came to roses. He and George Browne made a first class team. It was George's idea to have the rose nursery, but without Archie Tynedale's expertise, it would have come to nothing long ago.'

'Mollie seems to know what she's doing,' Shona commented.

'Yes, she certainly does, but she's more interested in arranging flowers than growing them when it boils down to it. Can you pass me that twine, please, love? Of course, that's one reason why your mother and Mollie get on so well together, having a common interest, isn't it? Oh it looks as if we've got a couple of customers. Could you serve, I'm a bit mucky and young Josh is busy watering.'

After Shona had dealt with the customers, she had a quick word with Josh Huggins, their hired hand as Mollie called him, and then collecting a pair of secateurs, went to select some roses for Jane's Florist.

This was one of her favourite occupations. She was spoilt for choice as usual. The colours ranged from pastel shades to deep ruby red. The scent was intoxicating. After a bit, she eased her aching back and, collecting up an armful of roses, went to put them in a bucket of water in one of the greenhouses.

Mollie Browne had arranged to collect Toby from school, as the village hall was nearby and so Shona decided to make her father, Josh and herself some tea. She was just walking past the hedge which bordered the rose nursery and Rose Lodge, when Mallory Tynedale appeared through the connecting gate. She stood gaping at him and he grinned.

'Sorry, if I startled you. My grandmother still has a key for emergencies . . . anyway, now I can kill two birds with one stone for a second time.'

'And good afternoon to you too!' she said, coolly. 'So what kind of emergency is this?'

For a moment he looked flummoxed

and then he laughed.

'Point taken. I promise I won't make a habit of creeping up on you. Is your father around? My grandmother was at the hairdresser's when he phoned about coming to see her tomorrow, and so she's sent me over to arrange a time. And the invitation still stands for you to see round the studio, of course.'

'Thanks, but that rather depends on whether I can be spared,' she told him, determined not to appear too eager.

'Right,' he said. 'We'll leave the invitation open.'

'He wondered if she'd just been polite on Sunday. Perhaps she wasn't interested in art. A pity, he'd have liked the opportunity to get to know her better.'

'Stand still,' he commanded. Startled she obeyed. He leant towards her and plucked some rose petals from her hair. A little shiver shot along her spine and she caught her breath, aware that this man attracted her.

'There, that's better. You have the

45

most beautiful hair,' he said in such a matter-of-fact tone that he might have been commenting on the weather. Well, she was immune to his flattery, she told herself, trying to ignore her quickening pulse and the woody scent of his cologne.

Whatever was the matter with her? She reminded herself that Adrian would be back in England before long.

Much to her relief, her father appeared at that moment and, with a muttered excuse, she escaped to the house.

'It's not fair!' Toby protested when Shona mentioned her invitation to visit Mallory's studio on the following afternoon. 'That means you're getting to go before me.'

'Well, I'm sure you'd rather wait and go with all your friends on Friday, wouldn't you?'

'I suppose . . . Mr Tynedale's going to show us how to do some sculpture.'

They'd all had their meal at Mollie's house that evening. She was an excellent cook and enjoyed their company.

'I thought it would only be a matter of time,' she remarked cryptically, as they helped her clear away the supper things.

'What would?' Shona asked, wondering what on earth she meant.

'Before Mrs Tynedale started putting

in her two pennorth.'

Shona stared at Mollie, but before she could question her any further, Kathleen Sutton intervened hastily.

'Mollie, we haven't said anything to Shona yet. We've left that to you.'

Mollie Browne busied herself at the sink. 'Oh, I don't mind Shona knowing. After all, she's one of us,' she said.

'Knowing what? This sounds serious. Come on, out with it!' Shona implored, anxious to know whatever was going on.

But Mollie wouldn't be hurried. She made a large pot of tea, checked that Toby was happily kicking a ball around in the garden, and then they all sat round the big pine kitchen table.

'You see, Shona, it's like this . . . '

Shona listened, her head in a whirl, as Mollie gave her a brisk and rather garbled run down of the state of the rose nursery's finances.

'My George was wonderful with roses, but he really didn't have much idea about running a business,' she concluded. 'By the time I realised he was in hot water, it was too late . . . '

'May I?' Mr Sutton butted in.

Mollie nodded. She poured more tea and pushed a plateful of chocolate biscuits towards them. Mr Sutton helped himself to a couple of chocolate fingers and waved them about to illustrate his point, as he spoke.

'You see, Shona, since her husband died, Mrs Tynedale has been what might be termed, a sleeping partner, in the rose nursery business. At one point, a few years back, when the business was on the verge of going under, Archie Tynedale poured quite a bit of money into it to keep it afloat.'

'He never asked for interest — said it was a long term investment,' Mollie explained. 'We already rented the land from the Tynedales, apart from the plot we bought to build this house on. My husband got us into rather a lot of debt, and as your father says, if it hadn't been for Archie Tynedale . . . '

'Well, I knew Mrs Tynedale owned a

share in the business, but . . . ' Shona began, looking at their sombre faces and wondering what other revelations there might be.

'She actually owns two thirds of the nursery, Shona, together with the land it stands on and Paddy's Field where your caravan's parked. It came as a shock to me when my George died and I discovered exactly what the situation was, I can tell you. As you know, your parents also own a 10% share which we sold to them with Archie's consent.'

'Go on . . . Shona urged.'

'After Archie Tynedale died, I thought, that's it! Mrs T will want interest from her investment at the very least. Anyway, nothing happened but now, I suppose the estate's been sorted and Mallory's here and taking a look around the place.'

Mollie's voice cracked with emotion and Kathleen put a reassuring arm on hers.

'Look, perhaps you're reading too much into the situation. After all, no-one's actually said anything, have they?'

'Veronica Tynedale's asked us to go over to look at her roses, and Shona said Mallory told her his grandmother hadn't shown any interest up until now. Supposing, now she's more her old self, she's decided she wants to sell her two thirds share. I couldn't raise that sort of money at my time of life, and you've tied most of your capital up in the floristry business, haven't you? And you've got a mortgage.'

'Look, we'll cross that bridge when we come to it,' Edward Sutton told her gently, and at that juncture, Toby came rushing into the kitchen asking for a drink, and they changed the subject.

As she prepared for bed that night, Shona had plenty to think about. She had often wondered why the rose nursery hadn't been brightened up. It always appeared to be a thriving concern, but she'd had no real idea of the financial problems that Mollie Browne had been struggling with until now.

After all, Edward Sutton was still several years off retirement age, and although he had his teacher's pension, he still had a mortgage on the bungalow and had poured most of his capital into both the florist shop and the nursery.

When Kathleen Sutton had originally taken on the work at Jane's Florist, it had been both to help out her daughter and as a supplement to their income, but now that Jane had died the situation had changed. It looked like being a lean few years.

An image of Mallory Tynedale came into Shona's mind. Her father had given him a tour of the nursery that afternoon and, apparently, he'd asked a few pertinent questions about the business side of things. Just what exactly was his motive? She wondered.

If only Rob hadn't gone away. Surely it was down to him to sort out his mother's affairs and not leave it to the rest of them. She told herself she was being unfair. He'd had enough to cope with and needed time to sort himself out.

Shona drifted in and out of sleep and, in the end, decided to get up early. It was a glorious morning. She had a quick shower, made breakfast and sat outside under the brightly coloured awning. She loved the caravan for it gave her a small modicum of independence, although she realised she might have to review the situation in the winter. A dreadful thought suddenly occurred to her. Supposing Mrs Tynedale decided to sell Paddy's Field!

★ ★ ★

The morning shot past in a usual hectic round of deliveries, taking orders and serving customers. After a coffee break, Shona went into the back of the shop to help her mother with some flower arrangements for a birthday party that evening.

'I did suggest we did them in situ,' Kathleen Sutton said worriedly, 'but it's a surprise party and they want everything delivered between six and seven o'clock tonight at the village hall.'

'Don't worry, Mum, I'll put off going to Rose Lodge this afternoon.'

'You will not! You deserve some free time. Providing you help me now, I'll manage. I'd appreciate it though, if you could lend a hand to set the arrangements out at the village hall this evening.' She lowered her voice. 'I could just wish young Kylie would pull her weight a bit more. Her heart's just not in this job. She spends half her time chatting to that boyfriend of hers on her mobile.'

'Then put your foot down,' Shona advised.

She managed to get away from the shop just before three o'clock, and hurried back to the caravan to tidy up.

'Are you ready, Shona?' her father called out presently, banging on the door.

Shona let him in and examined her reflection critically in the mirror.

'We mustn't keep Mrs Tynedale waiting,' Edward Sutton told her in his best schoolmaster's voice.

Shona picked up her keys. 'You're doing her a favour, Dad, just you remember that.'

Her father sighed, 'It doesn't hurt to be charitable now and again, Shona.'

'Even if Mollie Browne is right and Mrs T is getting Mallory to size up the business?'

'We don't know that for sure, love, although he was certainly asking a lot of questions concerning the nursery yesterday. Your mother and I had a bit of a sleepless night, after all that Mollie said.

We're fully aware that Veronica Tynedale will listen to Mallory — in the way that she listened to Archie and that, if Mallory advises her to pull out of the business, then she'll probably do just that.'

As they walked towards Rose Lodge, Shona thought of Paddy's field and her caravan. Her own little haven. She couldn't help wondering if their unsettled world might be about to change yet again.

Mallory Tynedale was waiting for them on the veranda and Mrs Tynedale joined them shortly afterwards. She was using a stick and leaned heavily on Mallory for support as they walked round the grounds.

Edward Sutton spent a bit of time surveying the roses in the rose-garden and then looked at several specimens nearer the house. He had gleaned a lot from George Browne over the past few years and had read up a fair amount as well.

'I don't think there's anything too much the matter,' he told Mrs Tynedale at length. 'One or two bushes need replacing but, for the most part it's just a question of pruning, spraying and so forth — mainly a job for the autumn. Perhaps I could come over and do a bit of cosmetic work on them, but I wouldn't want to upset Harry.'

'It doesn't take much to upset him these days, I'm afraid,' Mrs Tynedale told him. 'He hates change. When my husband became ill, Harry had to get used to taking his orders from me and, now that I'm finding it increasingly difficult to get around, he takes them from Mallory.'

Mallory grinned. 'Harry remembers me as a small boy in shorts who was always after his precious strawberries.'

Mrs Tynedale's face softened. 'My son, Thomas, was just the same, but Miranda never cared for them — said they brought her out in a rash.'

Presently, Mr Sutton and Mrs Tynedale disappeared into the conservatory to have a chat over a cup of tea and the house-keeper appeared with a covered basket, which she handed to Mallory, before vanishing indoors again.

'Shades of Little Red Riding Hood,' Shona commented with a grin, as they set off towards the studio.

A small ginger cat appeared from

nowhere and wound itself round his legs.

'Out of the way, Cimmi, or you'll trip us up!'

'Cimmi?' Shona asked, amused.

'Short for Cinnamon. We had to keep her out of the way whilst my sister was here. She can't stand cats.'

Now why didn't that surprise her? 'Well, I like them. I think they're great characters.'

Mallory unlocked a door leading into an outbuilding.

'Years back this was a stable block. Actually, we used to have a couple of ponies here when we were younger — rode them round Paddy's Field, but nowadays, we go over to the riding school near to Elaine Jennings if we want a hack. Anyway, come on in.'

He set the basket down on a table and switched on a kettle whilst she stood looking around her at the whitewashed walls adorned with colourful paintings.

'I'll show you round properly, in a minute. The rooms are not that large

59

but perfect for what I want, now if madam would care to be seated, tea will be served shortly, unless you prefer coffee?'

'Oh, but I wasn't expecting . . . '

He swept off the cloth with a flourish and placed it on the workbench and then proceeded to unpack the basket. There were scones with pots of cream and jam and he opened a container to reveal a quantity of luscious looking strawberries.

'Harry's pride and joy — only, nowadays, they're mine for the picking and I picked them myself this morning.'

As she sat enjoying the tea, Shona realised that any idea she might have had about tackling him about Mrs Tynedale's thoughts for the nursery, would have to be put on hold, She realised she'd have to go slowly or she wouldn't learn a thing.

She savoured the strawberries, thinking that either Mallory was a very clever man trying to soften her up before crunch time or Mollie Browne's suspicions were unfounded.

Shona Agrees To Help Mallory

'So, Shona, what did you do before you came here? Were you always in the floristry business?'

She shook her head and finished her mouthful of strawberries before replying. 'I'm not a complete novice because I used to work with my mother during my uni days. My mother's never owned her own business before but she's worked as a florist for many years. Actually, until recently, I was a project manager working mainly in parks and gardens and brown field developments up in London.'

'Sounds interesting — so are you here on a temporary basis just until Rob returns or what?'

She shrugged. 'We'll wait and see how things pan out. Anyway, what about you?'

He pushed the bowl of strawberries towards her. 'Help yourself — and you'd better eat some of these scones or my name will be mud.'

'At this rate I'll put on pounds.' She coloured as his gaze travelled over her.

'I can't believe that — anyway, to answer your question. I've come here for as long as it takes to help sort things out for my grandmother. Now she's feeling more up to it, we have to take a look at the future.'

'How d'you mean?' She spread a scone liberally with cream and put some jam on it.

'Now that's interesting, I always put the jam on first — like this.'

He was prevaricating and well she knew it! Obviously, her suspicions were right. He was trying the softly softly approach. 'Mallory, this tea is gorgeous and I really appreciate it, but I suspect there's something you're trying to tell me.'

He smiled and surveyed her, head on one side. 'I can think of plenty things I might say — after all, you're a very charming tea companion, but actually, I was wondering . . . '

'Yes?' she prompted, scone halfway to her mouth.

'My speciality — besides sculpture — is portrait painting . . . would you be prepared to sit for me?'

She gaped at him. This was the very last thing she had expected!

'Well, no-one has ever asked me before. I'm flattered.'

'You'd better wait until you've seen the finished result before you say that — so, will you?'

She paused, her heart beating a wild tattoo. 'I'd have to fit in around all the other things I've committed myself to,' she warned him.

'But of course — that goes without saying . . . more tea?'

She passed her cup, wondering if she were wise to become involved with Mallory. After all, earlier that same afternoon she'd told herself she was immune to his charms, but she couldn't deny that she found him attractive.

'So tell me, do you devote the entire day to your work here or it just a hobby?' she asked him now.

He chuckled. 'I only wish I could spend more time on it, but a guy's got to live. No, I'm an architect, mainly contract work for a couple of firms based in London. The joy of it is I can do a lot of the assignments from here. I've got everything I need and this is a very welcome bolt-hole. Now, if madam has finished perhaps she would like a guided tour.'

They began in the gallery, as he called it. The white-washed walls acted as a perfect foil for the selection of bright paintings and posters, whilst several display stand housed exquisite little sculptures of animals.

'How long did it take you to amass all this?' Shona asked in amazement. 'I didn't think you'd lived here for more than a few months.'

He placed a hand on her shoulder. 'Correct, but these aren't all mine, some of them are my father's and a number my grandfather's. We've all three got rather different styles. I'm hoping to have an exhibition at some point but, at present, my grandmother's still indecisive and, without her permission, I obviously can't go ahead. I came across a stack of paintings in the attic and it's taking for ever to clean them up. Some of them need framing but, fortunately, there's someone in the village who does that.'

'Let me guess which ones are yours.'

'That's easy. I've given you a clue.'

He took her arm casually and walked her across to a series of landscapes. 'These are my father's, beautiful, aren't they? They've been hidden away for far too long. Anyway, I must explain that I've been coming here on and off over the past few years and this project was my brainchild long before my grand-father died, although I only used the studio for my own work then.'

Shona was studying the leafy lanes and country views and then moved on to a series of garden scenes and several studies of roses, exquisitely executed and signed, *Archie Tynedale*.

'My grandfather was just as passion-ate about roses as George Browne, and I suspect your father feels the same way.'

She smiled. 'Yes, he certainly does. He loved his holidays here. George inspired him and he learned so much from him.' She watched for Mallory's reaction as she added, 'Of course, I'm aware your grandmother has a large stake in the rose nursery.'

His expression gave nothing away. 'Yes, my grandfather was full of surprises. He kept rather quiet about the fact that he'd owned twenty-five per cent from the outset and then, when George got into financial difficulties, he'd ploughed even more money into the business.'

Shona's eyes widened. 'Are you saying he didn't tell your grandmother?'

Mallory gave a wry smile. 'Not about the size of the investment. You see, he was quite closed about financial matters. Didn't want to trouble Grandma. Of course, Mollie knew a certain amount that was going on, but it still came as a big shock to her when she discovered by how much George was in debt.'

'Well, that won't happen again,' Shona reassured him. 'My father used to teach maths and he's very good on financial matters.'

'Yes, I'm sure he is. Anyway, let's leave it all to the experts, shall we? My grandmother has a very good solicitor and an equally good accountant and is more than happy to take their advice.'

Advice about what? Shona wondered uneasily. She followed Mallory round the gallery, her mind busily mulling over what he had said. His portraits were quite something. She stopped in front of one, open-mouthed. It was of a sultry-looking young woman with flowing black hair, dressed in a loose, low-cut garment.

'Is that Elaine Jennings?' she asked incredulously.

'Yes — oh, I suppose I ought to remove it for the time-being. She'll kill me if it's there when her pupils look round here tomorrow.'

'They probably wouldn't recognise her. She always power dresses and her hair is taken up. I had to do a double-take myself.'

He chuckled and, reaching up,

removed the painting. 'Ah, well, there's another side to most people.'

'So I'm beginning to find out,' she told him. 'And what would you expect me to wear if I sat for you? Not that I've decided yet.'

His eyes flickered. 'Well, if you do, then perhaps we could discuss it over a drink.'

He was a smooth talker, she'd give him that. 'We'll see,' she said. She concentrated on the pictures, trying to ignore her racing pulse.

'Is that a self portrait?' she asked, studying the picture keenly.

'What? Oh, no, that's a picture of my father, Thomas Tynedale. He wasn't too much older than I am when he died. I found a photograph and did it from that. Everyone tells me I look like him, so I suppose I have to believe them.'

'It must have been tough losing your father at such an early age.'

A shadow crossed his face. 'It was, in more ways than one, but my grand-parents were marvellous — that's why

I'd like to do all I can to help Grandma now. She deserves it.'

'She doesn't come over to the nursery any more,' Shona ventured.

'No, but I'm working on it. After all, she needs to keep an eye on her investments.'

'She always receives three monthly copies of the business accounts and is informed of anything else she needs to know about,' Shona put in quickly.

'Yes, I'm aware of that but, in the past, things were allowed to slide and my grandfather turned a blind eye. Anyway, perhaps I can take a look periodically.'

'You're entitled to do so, of course,' Shona agreed, 'although I feel sure both Mollie Browne and my parents would prefer to discuss things with your grandmother.'

'That's as may be, but she may well decide to let me deal with her business interests,' he told her rather curtly. 'Come on, let me show you the rest of this building.'

It was a spacious room — light and airy — furnished with everything he could possibly need for his work.

'This is amazing!'

'It is, isn't it? I'm pretty chuffed with it myself. Now when the kids come tomorrow, I'm thinking of letting them have some clay and getting them to make some animals. What d'you reckon?'

'Yes you can't go wrong with animals.'

He indicated the walls. 'I've got a few more posters to put up and some of the art work they've put together in their Friday club. Of course, Elaine wants to display it in school afterwards.'

'It's lovely to get the children involved. I know Toby's very keen.'

Lastly, he showed her his office; a small room very neat and professional-looking with some expensive looking computer equipment.

Shona was suitably impressed. 'You've really utilised these buildings, haven't you? But, if you're only here for a temporary period . . . '

His face was expressionless. 'Well, eventually, I'm hoping to hold an exhibition here — three generations of painters. Until then, I intend to make good use of it.'

She looked at her watch. 'I've promised my mother I'll help her set out some flower arrangements for a party at the village hall, so I'd best be going now. Thanks for tea and the tour. I'm sure the children will enjoy themselves tomorrow.'

As she made to move, he put out a hand and caught her arm, sending a little shiver dancing along her spine.

'Before you rush away, I was wondering if you'd care to come for that drink tonight?'

'I've told you I've arranged to help my mother in the village hall,' she said unsteadily.

'That won't take all the evening, will it?'

'You're very persistent. As I've already said, I haven't made my mind up about the portrait yet.'

His grey eyes held hers and a slight smile curved his lips. 'That's OK. I wasn't planning on starting it immediately. We can still have a drink, can't we? Let's say eight o'clock in the Malt Shovel.'

She knew she ought to refuse, but found herself accepting against her better judgement, telling herself that Elaine Jennings was probably tied up with schoolwork that evening and so Mallory was at a loose end.

'So how did you get on at the Tynedale's?' Kathleen Sutton asked her daughter as they began to set out the floral arrangements on the tables in the village hall.

Shona grinned. 'I had a wonderful strawberry tea, a conducted tour of Mallory's studio and we're meeting up for a drink tonight.'

Her mother gave her a keen look. 'Shona, you do know he's . . . '

'Friends with Elaine Jennings . . . yes, Mum, don't worry. I don't think a drink will hurt, do you?'

'No, of course not, dear.' Kathleen Sutton concentrated on her task. 'Elaine Jennings is such an elegant young woman, isn't she? And obviously very ambitious. I did hear she's only in her mid-thirties.'

Shona thought fleetingly of the

portrait in Mallory's studio.

'Hmm — that reminds me, we need to do something to help Toby improve his literacy skills.'

'Yes, your father's already said the same thing. I'm afraid spelling's not my strong point either,' Kathleen admitted.

'Perhaps Dad or I had better have a word with Mrs Jennings — get some holiday work for Toby.'

Toby was eating at a friend's house that evening and Mollie Browne had company, so there were just the three of them for supper at the bungalow.

'I've arranged to go over to Mrs Tynedale's place a couple of times a week, to sort out the roses,' Edward Sutton told them.

'Well, don't go overdoing it,' his wife cautioned. 'Did she give any hint as to any future plans?'

'Only that Rose Lodge was getting rather too much for her. She appreciates Mallory being there, but doesn't know how long he'll be able to stay. She seemed to be dropping a series of subtle hints without saying anything specific. What about you, Shona. Did you manage to glean anything from Mallory?'

Shona filled her parents in with the one or two comments Mallory had made regarding the nursery, but prudently avoid telling them that he wanted to paint her portrait.

'Perhaps we've been jumping to the wrong conclusions,' Edward Sutton said at length. 'I wouldn't say there was any major cause for concern.'

Kathleen Sutton relaxed visibly. 'Phew that's a relief — more vegetables, anyone?'

'I suppose we have to face up to the fact that no-one's getting any younger,' Shona remarked. 'I mean how much longer is Mollie going to want to run the nursery?'

Her parents stared at her. 'Thank you, Shona!' her mother said. 'Just as we're trying not to worry about one aspect, you throw another spanner in the works.'

'I'm just being realistic, that's all. All the time that Rob was prepared to help out of a weekend or in the evenings during busy times, that was one thing, but now the situation has completely changed.'

Her mother sighed and her father said, 'Look, let's not dwell on what might happen in the future, eh?'

As she helped her mother with the dishes, Mrs Sutton said, 'I don't want your father worried, Shona. He's hoping to go on working for a few years yet. There's been a lot of expense recently . . . I wasn't going to tell you this, but one of his investments hasn't been doing so well recently.'

'And now you're paying me a salary. Oh, Mum, why didn't you say something? Trust me to put my big foot in it.'

Her mother gave a rueful smile, wishing she hadn't had to mention it to her daughter.

'You go off and enjoy your evening. We'll think of some way round it. It's not as if we're on the breadline yet!'

Shona changed into a pair of dressy

black trousers and a kingfisher-blue, embroidered tunic top. She swept up her hair and added a pair of dangling earrings and some light make-up.

It was only a short drive to the Malt Shovel. Shona arrived early and, not fancying going in alone, sat at one of the picnic tables outside.

A few minutes later Mallory pulled up in his car. 'Sorry I'm late, Shona. My grandmother lost her television glasses, just as I was coming away, and there's a programme she particularly wanted to watch.'

He took he arm lightly and the contact was electric. There was no denying that he was an extremely attractive man.

'I like that blue thing you're wearing,' Mallory remarked, as they sat enjoying their drinks in a secluded alcove inside the pub. 'Something like that would be just what I had in mind for the portrait.'

He saw her expression and raised his hand. 'OK, I know I'm jumping the gun.'

Her features relaxed and she took a sip from her glass before replying.

'It would be a new experience for me, having my portrait painted, although I'm sure you could find plenty of other girls to model for you.'

A slight smile played about his mouth as he surveyed her.

'Oh, yes, they're all falling over themselves — I wish! My sister has refused point-blank — would you believe! Honestly, Shona, I'd be delighted. You're a very pretty girl. Of course, we must bring the flowers into it somehow.'

'You mean you want me to hold a rose between my teeth,' she teased and suddenly they were laughing together, as if they'd known each other for years.

★ ★ ★

The evening passed all too quickly. Mallory had thought he'd need to use all his powers of persuasion to get Shona to sit for the portrait, and was secretly surprised when she'd agreed.

He realised she was very much her own person and viewed him with a certain amount of suspicion, although he wasn't sure why.

'My grandmother tells me your parents used to come here on holiday and that's how they got to know the Brownes,' he said now.

'Yes, they started coming here when I was at uni — stayed with the Brownes for B and B. They love this area of Kent and it's a very good base for National Trust properties.'

'So they decided to put down roots here,' Mallory prompted gently.

'It was gradual,' Shona explained. 'Dad was becoming increasingly unhappy in the teaching profession and, when he learned his school was going to amalgamate with another one in the area, he opted for redundancy. It was like an answer to a prayer because he was finding the work so stressful.'

'He'd always loved his garden and was becoming increasingly interested in roses. George Browne wasn't in the best of health and that's when Dad offered to help out. At first, my parents lived in the caravan where I'm living now, and then the bungalow became vacant.'

'You live in the caravan on Paddy's Field?' Mallory asked in some surprise.

She nodded. 'Until the winter at any rate. It's convenient for work and it gives me a bit of freedom and independence.'

An odd expression flickered across his face and she wondered what thoughts were going through his mind.

He set down his drink and said slowly, 'Years back, my grandparents used to let one or two people use that field. I thought it was empty nowadays.'

'Well, it is, apart from the caravan. It'd made a great extension to the nursery, I suppose, but it's such a lovely spot that I hope that never happens.'

'It's where the pony used to be kept when Miranda and I were children. So Mrs Browne rents it along with the rest of the ground, does she?'

'Apparently so,' Shona told him and

he rubbed his chin, grey eyes serious.

'Well, you've certainly given me food for thought.'

Shona wondered what he meant, but he obviously had no intention of enlarging on it, and she decided it would be best not to question him for the present.

Shortly afterwards, she got to her feet saying she'd an early start the next morning, and he didn't persuade her to stay.

The following day was hectic from start to finish. In the morning, Shona and Kathleen went to do some flower arrangements in the church for a wedding and then, after lunch, Shona covered for her mother who had a hair appointment. Kylie suddenly developed a bad headache and Shona felt obliged to send her home, although she suspected that the girl wanted to get ready for a date with the latest boyfriend.

When Kathleen Sutton returned at four o'clock she insisted Shona went home too.

* * *

A short while later, Shona was sitting outside the caravan drinking a welcome cup of tea and gazing across the field which was strewn with a mass of wild flowers; poppies, ox-eye daisies, wild mallow and sweetpeas.

It would be devastating if the field had to go, but what if Mrs Tynedale had other plans for it? With just one caravan parked there, Shona's family would be hard-pressed to convince her that they really had need of it.

Suddenly Toby and Sammi came running towards her. Toby was carrying two large punnets of strawberries and Sammi had Mrs Tynedale's ginger cat in her arms.

'We've had a brill time and Mr Tynedale said we could have these because they were left over from our strawberry tea.' Toby carefully placed the strawberries on the picnic table.

'I'm glad you've enjoyed yourselves — did he let you in through the little gate?'

Toby nodded. Shona glanced at the squirming cat in Sammi's arms.

'What are you doing with that cat, Sammi? He belongs to Mr Tynedale.'

'I know, but he followed me. He's called Cimmi.'

'Cimmi, Sammi, Cimmi, Sammi,' Toby chanted. Meowing, Cimmi sprang out of the child's arms and shot under Shona's chair.

'Well, we'd better return him before he wanders off. What's happened to the rest of your group?'

'Most of their mums turned up to collect them and Mrs Jones is taking the rest back to school — she's one of the teaching assistants,' Toby explained, seeing Shona's puzzled expression. 'I told her Sammi's having supper with us — that's OK, isn't it?'

'Only if she phones her mum. You really ought to have checked first. Now run and find Grandpa for the key to the gate so that I can return this cat!'

She scooped up a protesting Cimmi and followed the children in the direction of the nursery. She got there just as Toby ran back with the key. After unlocking the gate he darted off again. She set down Cimmi and the affronted cat disappeared into the bushes.

Shona was just about to close the gate when the sound of laughter made her look through the gap. Mallory came into view with Elaine Jennings. They were deep in conversation and she was gazing at him earnestly.

As Shona watched, the head teacher caught at his sleeve and murmured something which made him laugh again. There was no mistaking the easy rapport the two of them had and Shona felt a sharp pang of envy.

She was in the middle of supper at the bungalow when the phone rang. Kathleen Sutton, being the nearest, went into the hall to answer it. When she returned there was a curious expression on her face. 'It's for you, Shona,' she told her daughter and paused.

Shona looked at her expectantly. 'What's wrong, Mum, is it bad news?'

'No, dear it's quite the reverse. It's Adrian — he's back in England!'

Life's Full Of Difficult Choices

Shona found her hand trembling as she picked up the receiver. 'Adrian! What a wonderful surprise! Why didn't you let me know you were coming back?'

'Oh, you know me — it all happened rather quickly at the end. Any chance we could meet up, say tomorrow?'

'Can't wait, but I'm working during the day, of course. How about the evening?'

'OK, supposing I pick you up at your parents' place around sevenish?'

They chatted for a few moments longer, and then he told her he'd have to go, as he was meeting up with some friends.

* * *

Shona spent most of the next day with her emotions in turmoil. She was totally unprepared for Adrian's sudden return. During the time that he'd been away, she had kept in touch, but in recent months, they hadn't communicated that much and she hadn't had a reply to her last letter or e-mails.

She wasn't sure how she felt about Adrian now. Absence was supposed to make the heart grow fonder, but he'd hurt her deeply when he'd announced his intention of doing a spell of V.S.O. with or without her.

At that time, she'd been convinced she was in love with him and had assumed that eventually they would marry and settle down happily ever after. But everything had to be put on hold when Jane died, and Shona had felt he was being unreasonable to go waltzing off to Africa like that, when she needed his support so badly herself.

Shona spent a long time getting ready for the evening. They were going to a fairly upmarket restaurant and she wanted to look her best. She glanced at herself critically in the mirror. She'd lost weight since Adrian had last seen her and could now fit into a dress that had been bought, on impulse, in a sale and discarded as being a little too tight. It was a classic style — a coffee-coloured linen shift which had not dated.

'So, how long have you been back in England?' Shona asked Adrian, as he drove her to the restaurant.

He looked a bit awkward. 'Almost five weeks.'

'Five weeks!' she echoed, unable to believe her ears. 'And you've only just got in touch.'

'I've been down to Devon, staying with my family,' he told her rather defensively.

'But that didn't prevent you from contacting me, did it?' Shona felt dazed and incredibly hurt. 'You didn't reply to my last letter or e-mail either.'

'Well, that's because I didn't receive them.' He turned into the restaurant car park.

'You see I had a bit of a holiday before I left Africa — must have gone before your mail arrived.'

It had not been a good start to the evening. Later as she sat opposite Adrian at their table, Shona realised they were behaving like strangers towards one another.

'So, how come you knew where to find me, if you didn't receive my correspondence?' she asked him now.

'Well, actually, your friend, Jill, told me where you were. I've been in London for a few days — called in at Hamden's.'

She stared at him. 'To find me or to see if there was any work?'

He hesitated slightly, and then reached out and caught her hands between his.

'Both, actually. Shona, you've no idea how much I've missed you. I've had the most amazing time in Africa and there's so much I want to share with you.' His pale blue eyes lit up. 'Wait till you see my photographs!'

A hovering waiter removed their empty plates. Shona tried to get her head round all this. Why had Adrian waited all this time before getting in touch? She took a sip of wine and, glancing towards the door, saw Mallory and Elaine Jennings arriving. He was unbelievably handsome in a dark suit and midnight blue shirt and she was looking amazing in a lime-green dress that showed off her curvaceous figure. Her glossy dark hair tipped her creamy shoulders. Shona turned her gaze away, wishing she hadn't seen them.

★ ★ ★

For the rest of the meal Adrian regaled Shona with stories of his time in Africa. He didn't seem to be that interested in knowing what she'd been up to. He was an amusing companion but he also liked to hold forth on his own pet themes and, after a while, she ceased to

91

listen. They had grown apart, she decided. She had been so looking forward to his return but now that he was here, sitting in front of her, she realised that one of the only things they'd had in common was their work.

From where she was sitting, Shona could catch a glimpse of Mallory and Elaine Jennings. They seemed to be enjoying themselves. To Shona's embarrassment, Mallory suddenly glanced in her direction. He had a glass in his hand and, smilingly, raised it in acknowledgement.

'Who's that?' demanded Adrian.

'Oh, just a neighbour,' Shona said airily. 'So what are your plans for the future? Are you hoping to get another spell in Africa or are you staying in England?'

After all, surely she had a right to know, or did he care so little about her that she didn't figure in his future plans?

'Whoa, give me a chance — I've only just got back!' he protested laughingly.

For a few moments they ate in silence and then he set down his knife and fork.

'That was excellent! This place is quite something!'

And suddenly Shona realised she'd probably been thoughtless in bringing him here.

'Adrian, I'm sorry — I'd forgotten you've been on a limited income these past months — we'll go dutch.'

He laughed. 'I'm OK, Shona. I came back to discover I'd had a pretty good tax rebate, plus building society interest — and I start work on Monday.'

Her eyes widened. 'At Hamden's?'

'Yep — they've welcomed me back with open arms. Admittedly I've only got a temporary contract to start with but . . . '

'Well, good for you,' she said, suddenly feeling a pang of nostalgia for her old job at Hamden's. Now that Adrian was going to be back in London, it seemed ironic that she was here in Woodhurst.

'So who are you staying with?'

'My friend, Jamie, and his wife. What a pity you're stuck here.'

Something in his tone made her say sharply, 'For your information, I like it here and anyway, it was my choice to come. I couldn't hang about on the off-chance that you might just happen to return from Africa and look me up.'

Adrian was taken aback. 'That's a bit below the belt, Shona!'

She shrugged. 'My family might run a rose nursery, but I can assure you life isn't exactly a bed of roses. We've had a terrible time these past months and it's not over yet. We're still facing problems. At present our top priority is to make life as secure and stable as possible for Toby. As I told you in my letters, my brother-in-law's taken a job abroad, so we need to be there for Toby. That's not that easy when we're also trying to run a couple of businesses.'

Adrian looked genuinely sympathetic. 'I'd no idea how difficult things had become, Shona. So how long's Rob away for?'

'I'm not too sure. It's all a bit uncertain — a few months to begin with.'

'Tough. You'll have to come up to London to see the old crowd.'

A waiter whipped away their plates and presented them with the dessert menu.

They both decided to settle for coffee and went into the lounge. They had to walk past Mallory's table and he called out a pleasant, 'Hi there,' but Elaine Jennings kept silent, although Shona was aware she was looking curiously at Adrian.

The rest of the evening passed pleasantly enough, but somehow it was as if the old magic and easy going relationship Shona and Adrian had once enjoyed was gone.

When she had told him about living in the caravan, he had seemed surprised, saying he'd always thought of her as someone who loved her creature comforts too much to rough it, as he put it. She supposed that he was alluding to her reluctance to accompany him to Africa.

It was still fairly early when he drove her back to her parents' bungalow, but he declined her invitation to come in. Leaning over he gave her a light kiss, promised to be in touch before too long, and was gone.

Shona stood there on the drive for several minutes, her eyes brimming with tears, as she realised that things were no longer the same between Adrian and herself.

The following morning Mollie took Toby to visit her sister. Shona accompanied her mother to church as usual, but they decided there was too much to do in the nursery to stay on for coffee.

Shona was glad to be kept occupied. There was a steady trickle of customers, making it impossible for the Suttons to eat a family lunch together. Presently, Shona volunteered to hold the fort so that, her parents, at least, could have a well deserved break.

By two o'clock, however, the nursery seemed deserted so Mrs Sutton insisted that Shona took the rest of the day off, as they intended to close at three o'clock, anyway.

After lunch, Shona escaped to the caravan. She changed into shorts and a sun top and sat with her legs outstretched, soaking up the sunshine and reading a magazine. A slight sound made her turn round, startled. Mallory Tynedale was surveying her from the hedge.

'Your mother said I'd find you here. I'm in a bit of a jam — a strawberry jam actually — and I thought you might be able to help me out.'

Shona, her peace shattered, glared at him coldly. 'I haven't got the remotest idea of what you're talking about!'

He grinned, and squatted on the grass beside her. 'My grandmother's invited some friends from The Beeches Residential Home to tea. It's Mrs Huggins' afternoon off, as you know, and she's left everything ready but, I'm in disgrace because I used up all the strawberry jam when the kiddies came for their picnic on Friday. Apparently, Mollie Browne always keeps us supplied, but she's out with Toby and your mother doesn't like to raid her larder. Anyway, she suddenly remembered you'd got a jar.'

Shona nodded. 'Mollie gave me one

of raspberry and one of strawberry when I moved in.' She got to her feet, 'I haven't opened either yet, so you can take your pick.'

He chuckled. 'Not the raspberry — apparently it plays havoc with elderly folks' dentures!'

Shona laughed too. 'The strawberry it is then — I'll go and fetch it.'

'I don't suppose . . . no, that would be too much to ask.' He looked at her appealingly.

'Go on . . . '

'Well I sort of volunteered my services to help out. You wouldn't . . . '

'Lend a hand?' she finished for him. 'Well, why not? It's not as if I'm doing anything else. You'll have to give me a few minutes to change though.'

He checked her out. 'And I was just thinking what a nice outfit that was.'

She coloured and disappeared into the caravan. Ten minutes later she emerged, looking demure in a white top and blue cotton skirt, her hair neatly secured with a piece of ribbon.

She set down the jar of jam on the table and looked around for Mallory who was on the far side of the field. He came hurrying across.

'Just having a little mosey round the field. It's delightful, isn't it?'

'Yes, I think so. I'll just tell my parents where I'm going — in case they need me for anything.'

Mr Sutton was watering the stock and raised his hand. Shona hurried up to him and explained what was happening and then caught up with Mallory at the gate.

'So Toby's out with Mollie Browne today,' he remarked, as they set off along the path. 'It's good he's got so many people to look out for him.'

'We do our best to make his life secure and happy,' Shona told him.

'It must be difficult fitting everything in — especially your social life . . . Does your, er, friend live locally?'

Shona didn't want to discuss Adrian. 'He's up in London — works at the firm I've recently left,' she told him shortly and, fortunately, he didn't pursue it.

Mrs Tynedale was sitting on the terrace looking anxious.

'Thank goodness, Mallory. I thought you'd gone to make that jam!'

He chuckled. 'I've returned with reinforcements, Gran.'

Mrs Tynedale smiled at Shona. 'This is kind. Mrs Huggins has left most things ready, but an extra pair of hands would be most welcome. And it looks as if you've arrived not a moment too soon — here come our guests!'

It was a hectic but enjoyable couple of hours. Mrs Tynedale's friends — two elderly ladies and an old gentleman, had come with a female carer who volunteered to preside over the teapot.

* * *

As everyone tucked into dainty sandwiches and finely sliced fruit bread in the dining room, Shona darted into the kitchen, split the scones and arranged them on plates, whilst Mallory put the jam into cut-glass dishes and ladled some cream into a couple of bowls, for those who were able to digest it.

They loaded the tea trolley and pushed it into the dining room to find everyone chattering away nineteen to the dozen, whilst they tucked into the repast with obvious pleasure. A mound of strawberries already provided a centre piece on the table, and, in addition to the scones, there was a lemon drizzle cake and a Victoria sandwich.

'We all enjoy it at The Beeches,' said a little lady called Betty. 'We have good fun, don't we, Sylvia?'

Her silver-haired friend nodded agreement. 'We have exercises on two mornings a week, bingo once a month and a wonderful sing-song. They have different kinds of entertainment. Last week it was a magician.'

Mrs Tynedale visibly winced.

'They've got satellite TV,' the elderly gentleman piped up, helping himself to a scone.

'Henry likes his television, don't you, Henry,' cooed the carer.

'Sometimes we have outings to the seaside,' Sylvia added. 'I think you'd enjoy it, Veronica, and you'd never feel lonely.'

'I've got my budgerigar,' Betty said. 'He's great company.'

When Henry burst into song over the strawberries and cream, Shona caught Mallory's eye and tried hard not to laugh. The old gentleman was an absolute character, she decided.

★　★　★

Afterwards, as Mallory helped settle her guests in the car, Mrs Tynedale said to Shona, 'I'm so grateful to you, my dear, for stepping into the breach. I think it all went off splendidly, don't you? As you must have gathered, my family are worried about me living on my own in this big house. I have to admit that I've been a bit lonely since Archie died but, you know, I'm not sure that I'm ready for a residential home just yet.'

'Wouldn't your daughter-in-law come and live here?' Shona asked tentatively.

Veronica Tynedale sighed, 'Oh, no, my dear. Selena and I don't exactly hit it off. I'm afraid we wouldn't last for more than a week under the same roof. I'd hate to sell the old place, but I'm afraid it might come to that sooner rather than later. Miranda wouldn't wish to live here either and Mallory — well I'm always hopeful he'll marry one day, but it wouldn't be fair for his wife to take on his grandmother too!'

They waved as the carer finally drove the elderly folk away.

'Of course, I had hoped that if Mallory and Elaine made a go of it, but whilst she's very good with children, she doesn't seem to have much time for senior citizens. She made it very clear that she was fully occupied this afternoon.'

Shona murmured something appropriate. However could she have imagined she'd been Mallory's first choice, when

Elaine Jennings was always going to have first refusal?

'Well, that went well, didn't it? They all seemed to enjoy themselves,' Mallory remarked, as he joined them. 'Now I could do with some tea. I'm absolutely parched.'

'You go ahead, dear. I'm going to have a little rest. There's a television programme I particularly wanted to see,' his grandmother said. 'Now you make a good tea, Shona. You deserve it. I've suddenly realised, the two of you were so busy looking after the rest of us that you didn't have time for any yourselves, did you?'

Shona had been going to make her excuses and escape, but now she felt she couldn't without offending Mrs Tynedale. As she sat in the garden in the last of the afternoon sunshine, she decided that perhaps the direct approach was best.

'Your grandmother was telling me that she's considering leaving here.'

Mallory set down his teacup. 'Not

immediately and only when she's found somewhere suitable to move to. It has to be her decision.'

'Of course, and none of your family wants to keep the house on?'

'It's not as simple as that.' He leant back in his chair, hands behind his head. 'My late father adored this place and I don't doubt that — if he'd still been alive — then he would have persuaded my mother to live here — but, as things are, she's not too far from Miranda in Hertfordshire. Miranda's got a new man in her life so she's not likely to move back here.'

'I see, and what about you?' Shona asked, meeting his gaze.

Mallory swallowed his tea and reached for another scone. 'Well, I love this old place, but I'm afraid it's not that straightforward. Anyway, we're considering all the options.'

Shona took a deep breath. 'So, you think Mrs Tynedale might have to sell up then?' There! She'd asked the question now.

There was a long pause and then Mallory said, 'It's complicated, Shona. You see my grandfather stated in his will that, all the time my grandmother wished to live at Rose Lodge, then nothing would change. However, if she decided to sell up then half the proceeds from her entire estate would go to her, but the rest would be divided between Miranda and myself. Of course, we'd make sure that she had enough to live on for the remainder of her days, but . . . '

Shona stared at him as his words sank in. 'And by the estate do you mean absolutely everything?'

Mallory nodded. 'The house and all the grounds and, I'm afraid that includes Paddy's Field.'

'I see,' Shona said dully. She felt her throat constricting. He hadn't mentioned the nursery, but surely he would know that the land it stood on belonged to the estate too?

Mallory speared a strawberry. 'We thought Gran might like the idea of going into The Beeches, although the fees are astronomical. Actually, it was Elaine who suggested it. A neighbour of hers was there for a few weeks, recuperating from an operation.'

Everything slotted into place now, Shona thought grimly. Whilst Veronica Tynedale might not relish the idea of living in The Beeches, if she could be persuaded to go there then that would probably suit Elaine Jennings very well indeed.

Shona hurriedly finished her tea and popped into the house to say goodbye to Mrs Tynedale who had switched off the TV and was sitting staring into space.

'Thank you for coming, dear. You know, I really don't think I should like going to The Beeches but, at the moment, I can't see any alternative. It's no joke getting old.'

Shona had a lot on her mind as she made the short journey back to the nursery.

Later when she recounted her conversation with Mallory and Veronica Tynedale to her parents, her mother said, 'Well, we'll cross that bridge when we come to it, shall we?' While her father, with his own particular brand of wisdom, remarked, 'Never trouble trouble, till trouble troubles you.'

As she helped her mother clear away the supper things, Shona said, 'It's no good us burying our heads in the sand, Mum. Mallory hasn't mentioned the rose nursery yet, but we need to be prepared.'

Mrs Sutton stacked the plates tidily. 'Shona, I've told you not to bother your father with these matters. When and if the matter arises, then we'll deal with it. Until then, let's just take each day as it comes, shall we?'

And Shona had to accept that she

was going to have to shoulder this particular burden on her own for the time-being.

* * *

The next couple of days were so busy that Shona didn't have time to dwell on things. There was a big funeral on the Tuesday morning and Jane's Florist had had several floral tributes to make up and deliver, and then there was an equally big fiftieth wedding anniversary dinner at a local hotel and they had been asked to do the flowers.

Shona was delighted to be given the task of arranging the smaller table decorations, whilst her mother concentrated on the larger one for the centrepiece. They also arranged several vases of flowers at the hotel.

'There, what do you think?' Mrs Sutton asked when they had finished their task.

The tables were a triumph, glistening with glass and shining cutlery. The damask napkins were golden, and the floral arrangements of cream and gold roses with just a touch of fern sprayed gold to match, looked magnificent. For the vases, they had chosen taller cream lilies and delicate golden-yellow carnations, interspersed with some long-stemmed golden roses.

The hotel manager came over, as they were preparing to leave. 'We often have functions in this room and frequently the guests leave the flowers to us. We also require fresh arrangements weekly in the dining room and reception area. Just recently we haven't been too happy with our current florists. I was wondering if you might be interested in taking over the job?'

'Well, that was an unexpected accolade!' Mrs Sutton said, as they drove back to the shop. 'I just hope we can fulfil all these additional commitments!'

On Wednesday evening, Shona found herself roped in to assist her mother and Mollie Browne at the W.I. where they had agreed to give a flower arranging demonstration, together with a short talk on floristry. It went extremely well and afterwards, as the ladies came forward to examine the various arrangements on display, Shona was surprised to see Elaine Jennings amongst them.

'I did so enjoy your talk, Mrs Sutton,' the headmistress told her. 'I was wondering if I might ask a favour?'

Mrs Sutton smiled. 'What can I do for you?'

'As I'm sure you're aware, it's our school fayre on Saturday afternoon.'

'Yes, Mrs Browne is running a plant stall and I was going to help her — don't tell me you want me to help on the white elephant stall instead!'

'Oh, no, it's nothing like that,' Elaine Jennings assured her seriously. 'The thing is the children have a little exhibition area — pictures, and such like. Some of them have entered in the flower classes so I was wondering if you'd be prepared to judge them for us?'

'Well, I'll be working at the shop in the morning and then helping Mrs Browne set up her stall from half past one, so I'm afraid I'll be rather occupied, but I'm sure Shona would oblige,' Mrs Sutton told her pleasantly.

Elaine Jennings hesitated slightly before saying, 'Well, that's a kind offer. Shall we say one o'clock?'

Shona, somewhat taken aback and feeling rather cornered, agreed and then her mother added quietly, 'Perhaps you could return the favour, Mrs Jennings? I realise that this is neither the time nor the place to discuss the matter, but before the end of term, one of us would like to see you regarding some holiday work for Toby.'

Elaine Jennings immediately became

very businesslike. 'I see. Normally, of course, the first port of call would be to talk with his class teacher — although with it being so near to the end of the school year, perhaps the consultation should be with me. I had assumed Mrs Browne was Toby's guardian whilst her son is away. I'm loath to discuss a child's progress with anyone other than the appointed guardian.'

'Actually, my husband is named, but we all pitch in and I feel sure my daughter would deal very adequately with Toby's educational matters,' Mrs Sutton said politely, but firmly.

When Elaine Jennings had gone, Mrs Sutton turned to some of the other ladies clustered around the table.

During the short drive home, she commented, 'That lady tests my patience to its limit. Instead of being supportive she continually puts obstacles in the way. Who does she think she is?'

Shona chuckled. 'I imagine you're talking about Elaine Jennings? I understand she's an excellent headteacher but, unfortunately, she finds it difficult to switch off, doesn't she?'

Except when she's with Mallory, Shona added silently. 'Thinking about the fayre — how's Toby's costume coming along for the fancy dress parade?'

'Well, we've finally dissuaded him from going as Harry Potter,' Mollie told her. 'It would have been easy, but just about every boy who's entered will be doing that, and so he's agreed to accompany Sammi, who's going as Wendy from Peter Pan. He's opted for Captain Hook.'

Shona laughed and her mother added, 'We've sorted him out with most things except for the wig — any ideas?'

The following evening Adrian rang up and Shona arranged to meet up with him in London on Friday night. She told him she'd need to be back early on Saturday morning. She rang her friend, Jill, to see if she could put her up on Friday night. Although, Jill readily agreed and said she was fine, Shona didn't think her friend sounded quite her usual self and wondered why.

Shona was just about to put the phone down when she had a sudden inspiration. Jill used to take part in amateur dramatics and still had some props and costumes so Shona asked if she could borrow a wig for Toby.

★ ★ ★

A slight frown creased Kathleen Sutton's forehead when Shona told her she'd be spending Friday night in London.

'Don't worry, Mum, I'll be back before you've even missed me,' Shona reassured her. 'I haven't forgotten we've got a busy agenda tomorrow.'

'Did I say anything? It's absolutely none of my business if you burn the candle at both ends.'

'And because you haven't asked, I'll tell you. I'm spending the evening with Adrian and staying overnight with Jill. Adrian's lodging with his friend, Jamie, and his wife and two children. There wouldn't be any room for more visitors.'

Kathleen Sutton smiled. 'Well, have fun, darling!'

'I will,' Shona grinned and kissed her mother on the cheek.

Arriving in London, she made her way over to Jill's flat to deposit her overnight bag and freshen up. Jill seemed pleased to see her, but Shona got the distinct impression that there was something on her mind. They sat over mugs of tea and biscuits, catching up on the gossip until Adrian put in an appearance, but Jill did not confide in her friend.

Adrian had booked a table at an Italian restaurant and over their pasta they chatted about their respective weeks, but Shona realised once again how wide apart their worlds had become.

Hamden's and her dreams and ambitions had already begun to fade into the background. It was a much slower pace of life in Woodhurst and Shona was beginning to realise what had attracted her parents to the village.

As they ate their dessert, Adrian told her how once he'd saved sufficient money, he intended to do another stint in Africa.

'It's a wonderful continent, in spite of all the deprivation. There's so much work to be done there. The children have so little and we have so much.'

Shona nodded. 'I admire you for what you want to do, Adrian, although I'm still not sure I could do it myself. I get the feeling that you're already champing at the bit to go back again.'

He smiled. 'You always could read me like a book, Shona. This country seems so materialistic after Africa. I had to come back, if only to convince myself that my motives for being there were the right ones. If only you'd come with me, then I'm sure you'd feel the same way.'

Shona stared at him. 'Adrian, we've been through all this a thousand times. You know why I can't go with you, at present. I've got family commitments!'

'Right, so Rob's gone swanning off and left you to cope with Toby. If you'd refused, what would have happened then?'

'Oh, I don't know,' she said wearily. 'I just don't think I'm cut out for VSO — not everyone is, you know. I realise it's a worthy cause, and I'll support you in any way I can, but, for the present, you'll have to accept that I intend to stay right here, in England.'

Shona wondered if he'd invited her here so that he could have another go at trying to persuade her to go back to Africa with him. Deep down, she recognised that Jane's death had drawn her family even closer together. Family meant a lot to her and she didn't want to be too far away from them, at present. She also realised that — if she truly loved Adrian — she would have agreed to go to the ends of the earth with him.

The evening was pleasant enough and when they'd finished their meal, Adrian asked Shona if she wanted to go on to a night club. She said no and so they wandered along hand-in-hand by the Thames, with all the other couples. She hoped that, perhaps, they could recapture some of that original spark but, even when he took her in his arms and kissed her, she realised that he was not awakening any deep feelings within her.

'I've missed you,' he told her, as he stroked her hair. 'Please think again. We'd have a great life together in Africa.'

'Have you ever considered that, perhaps, you're the one who needs to rethink?' she asked him.

Releasing her abruptly, he looked at her in genuine astonishment. 'How d'you mean?' he demanded.

'If you really cared about me, instead of putting your own plans first, you'd consider my situation. I've been prepared to put my entire career on hold because I recognise that there are other things in life besides ambition. Yes, what you do in Africa is very worthwhile so don't think I'm belittling it, but surely you could wait a while, until things have sorted themselves out in my life, before you start thinking about returning.'

He tensed and she knew she'd gone too far.

'You know what, Shona, I think I've made a lucky escape! If we'd got married, it could have ended up being the biggest mistake of my life! I love my family, don't think I don't, but with you it seems to be a case of marry me, marry my family!'

'That's a perfectly hateful thing to say. You've changed, Adrian. You know what your problem is? You just can't bear the thought that I'm not prepared to fall in with your plans, can you?'

They travelled in virtual silence back to Jill's flat, both lost in their own thoughts.

Jill was surprised to see Shona back so soon and, taking one look at her face, poured her a glass of wine.

'Come on, tell me what's happened. I take it Adrian's not coming in. Have you two come to blows, or what?'

Shona filled her in, carefully choosing her words and fully expecting her friend to be sympathetic. Jill surprised her, however, by telling her:

'You know I can see both sides. Neither of you is being particularly fair to the other. Who knows, by the time Adrian's saved enough money to enable him to go on his next trip, things might have swung round sufficiently for you to be able to leave your family and join him. After all, a relationship is based on give and take.'

Shona stared at her friend in surprise. 'What exactly are you trying to say?'

'Well, you had the choice to go with Adrian before you were ever needed in Woodhurst. If that arrangement had been made, would you have broken your contract and returned to England early?'

'Well, probably not, but I would have been home by now anyway, so what's your point?'

'Life's full of difficult choices. It was Rob's decision to leave his son with his grandparents whilst he went abroad to sort himself out. If, in a few months' time he came back and you were no longer needed in Woodhurst, then you'd be free to go with Adrian, but would you make some other excuse?'

She considered, 'Actually, I've already been thinking along those lines.' She sipped her wine. 'Perhaps the feelings I have for Adrian are not as strong as I thought they were. These past months have helped me put things into perspective. Both of us have been on a learning curve and we've matured, but it seems as if we've grown away from each other in the process.'

Jill looked thoughtful. 'Then surely it's just as well you've found out now — sooner rather than later. Actually, Shona, three's something I've got to tell you, because it's evident Adrian hasn't mentioned it.'

'That sounds ominous — what is it?' Shona asked curiously.

'On Monday, Adrian stepped into your shoes at Hamden's. He's got your old job on a year's contract, Shona.'

There was a silence whilst Shona took the significance of this on board. It was obvious now, that this was what had been bothering Jill.

At last Shona said, 'Well, I suppose someone had to get it, but I can't imagine why Adrian couldn't have come clean and told me it was him. He had plenty of opportunity to do so this evening.'

Jill didn't say anything further and, shortly afterwards, Shona went to bed, aware that she had an early start the following morning. Unfortunately, she had a rather sleepless night, as things buzzed around in her head.

There was something she couldn't quite grasp and suddenly she shot up in bed, as she realised what it was. Her job had been advertised before she left Hamden's. In order for Adrian to have been appointed so quickly, someone must have tipped him off about it being available.

A Surprising Business Meeting

All the way back to Woodhurst, Shona kept thinking about the conversation she'd had with Jill over breakfast that morning. When she had broached the subject of Adrian taking over her job at Hamden's, Jill has looked rather sheepish and then she'd mumbled, 'Actually, I told him about it, Shona. You see I've kept in touch with him all the time he's been in Africa.'

Shona had been somewhat taken aback. 'But you've never said anything. Wait a minute — you must have known he was back in England before I did!'

Jill had had the grace to look embarrassed. 'He stayed with Jamie for a couple of nights before leaving for Devon. Jamie mentioned about your leaving Hamden's and so naturally,

Adrian rang me to find out what was going on. That's when I told him about your job being advertised and suggested he applied for it. I wasn't to know he didn't intend to contact you until he returned from Devon.'

Shona watched the countryside whizzing by and tried to reason with herself. After all, she had given up her job, so why should it matter that Adrian had got it — albeit on a temporary basis?

She told herself that it wouldn't have done, if he'd rung her, because then she'd have told him about the post herself — even suggested that he applied for it. The way Adrian had gone about it, however, seemed rather underhanded and not the sort of behaviour she would have expected from him. Why hadn't he mentioned it the previous evening?

* * *

Mrs Sutton looked up with a sigh of relief as Shona entered the shop. 'Am I glad to see you! We've got a rush on and there are the deliveries still to do. Now, before I forget, have you got the wig for Toby? Shona, please don't tell me you've forgotten!'

Shona had clapped her hand to her mouth, as she visualised the blue carrier bag in which the black curly wig had been placed, standing by the sofa in Jill's sitting room.

'Mum. I'm so dreadfully sorry, but in the rush of getting away, I've left it behind. Whatever are we going to do?'

'Oh, we'll think of something,' Mrs Sutton said in her most placid tone. 'Any bright ideas, Kylie?'

'There's a fancy dress shop in the town,' Kylie said brightly.

'Nice one, Kylie, I'll go and get the yellow pages.' And Shona darted off.

A phone call confirmed that the shop had got a selection of wigs for hire.

'There's only one thing for it, Shona,' Kathleen Sutton told her daughter. 'You'll have to combine it with the deliveries — oh and I've promised to drop these roses off at the church for the ladies who are on the flower rota. Now, it's ten-thirty — can you be back here not a minute later than eleven forty-five, so that Kylie can have her lunch break before you go to do the judging?'

Thankfully, Shona drove off, wondering how she could have been so stupid. She completed the deliveries in record time, dropping off the roses on the way, and then parked in the nearby town which was bustling with shoppers.

There was a street market and she would have loved to linger. Fortunately, the fancy dress shop had just the wig Toby needed and Shona handed over what seemed an exorbitant sum of money, telling herself it was worth every penny.

She was taking a short cut back to the car park along an alley-way, swinging the carrier bag, when she nearly cannoned into Mallory Tynedale coming from the opposite direction. His arm shot out and steadied her, making her pulse race inexplicably.

'Hey, slow down! I've been running a few errands for my grandmother. Have you got time for a coffee?'

'Not really. Oh go on, I'm sure a few minutes won't hurt.'

He steered her back along the alley and into a street that ran parallel, where there was a coffee shop at the back of a baker's.

'Come on, choose a cake,' Mallory invited.

Shona studied the mouth-watering display. 'You're always feeding me, but they look delicious and breakfast was a bit sketchy and a long time ago.'

★   ★   ★

As they sat over coffee and sticky buns, Shona told Mallory the story of the wig. He gave a bellow of laughter, which incurred disapproving glances from the two elderly ladies at a nearby table.

'Isn't it dreadful the riff raff this place attracts?' he remarked, winking at

132

Shona and they both dissolved into mirth again. Regretfully, after a quarter of an hour, she got to her feet. 'Thanks, you've no idea how much better I feel for that. I must get my skates on now, I've got to relieve Kylie for her lunch break.'

'Don't forget your wig,' he said loudly, for the benefit of the two elderly ladies, who shot them a startled look.

Mallory accompanied Shona to the car park, and she drove back to Woodhurst in a much happier frame of mind, to find her mother champing at the bit.

'Oh, there you are, Shona. I was beginning to wonder where you'd got to. Did you get it?'

Shona produced the wig from her bag with a flourish, much to the amusement of a customer who had come into the shop to purchase a bunch of flowers.

Mrs Sutton attempted to explain, whilst she wrapped the flowers. Kylie removed her tabard and, grabbing her bag, thankfully left the shop. Shortly afterwards, Mollie Browne arrived with Toby, and Shona's mother hurried off to join them.

The next three quarters of an hour was hectic, and Kylie was five minutes late getting back to Jane's Florist. Shona hastily tidied herself and set off in the van for Toby's school.

Elaine Jennings was standing in the entrance hall, looking every inch a headmistress in a fashionable green trouser suit. She marched Shona off at a rapid pace across the playing field and into a small marquee which housed the children's work, and then hovered about whilst Shona deliberated over the delightful exhibits.

Shona took her time, entranced by the simplicity of the children's work and finding it quite a challenging task to select the winners.

'It's OK, Mrs Jennings — if you've got things to do, I'll be perfectly all right on my own,' Shona assured her, but the other woman remained where she was, as if waiting for someone. A few minutes later, Mallory turned up.

'Sorry, Elaine — a slight hitch. I'm afraid I lost track of time doing a job for my grandmother. Ah, Miss Sutton, we meet again. Has Elaine roped you in to do some judging too?'

Elaine Jennings murmured something Shona didn't catch, and just then a small child appeared in the entrance and told her headmistress that the celebrity who was coming to open the fête had arrived and, with a muttered apology, Mrs Jennings left.

'You mustn't mind Elaine. She can be a bit overbearing at times. It's her job and she's a bit of a perfectionist,' Mallory said.

Eventually, Shona awarded first prize to the creator of a charming arrangement of a maypole, which was obviously made from a kitchen towel centre covered in variegated ivy. The ribbons were represented by daisy chains, and a small jar of wild flowers, standing in a cardboard cut-out of grass, provided the background.

The older children had made gardens in dishes and these were decidedly easier to judge. Some of the entries were sophisticated and had evidently had a helping hand from an adult.

Shona selected a delightfully simplistic arrangement. The names had been placed inside envelopes which Elaine Jennings had instructed her to open only when the final choices had been made.

Mallory grabbed her arm. 'Come and help me decide. The portraits are no problem, but this garden design section is more up your street. What d'you reckon to this one?'

'We'll get shot at dawn, if we're caught conferring!' she warned him.

'Who's to know?' He dropped a casual arm about her waist, sending a little frisson shuddering along her spine. She agreed on his choice for first prize, but felt that the second and third places should have been the other way round.

'Great! That's settled. Now just look at this portrait. The children were asked to draw someone they knew . . . '

Shona laughed as she saw the picture of Elaine Jennings. The boy who had drawn her had got her off to a tee. 'That's excellent — oh, only second prize!'

'Yes, because the winner is definitely the little girl who drew this picture of her grandmother. Just look at her expression, it's priceless! Have you got to go back to the shop now?'

Shona consulted her watch. 'No, I've got time to see the fancy dress parade. I've promised Toby and Sammi I'd stay and, after all that kerfuffle with the wig this morning, I can hardly miss it, can I?'

Shona was so aware of the man standing beside her — of the spicy scent of his cologne and his sheer maleness. It seemed as if he had a magnetic quality about him. Adrian's back now, she told herself firmly. No more casual dates. It would be disloyal.

'I was wondering if we could fix a time for your first portrait sitting? How about next Wednesday afternoon?'

She's momentarily forgotten about the portrait and a promise was a promise, wasn't it?

'Suits me — I'd need to check with my mother, of course, in case I've overlooked anything important, but unless I phone you, I'll be there.'

'Great. Shall we say around three o'clock?'

'Yep — that sounds okay to me — now let's go and take a look at the fancy dress parade, before we miss it!'

★ ★ ★

At least two dozen children had entered the parade. As Mollie and Kathleen had surmised there were a good half a dozen Harry Potters, to say nothing of several Hermiones and one delightful red headed Ron. In addition, there were a fair number of characters from T.V.

programmes like Dr Who and Robin Hood.

Toby made a wonderful Captain Hook in an old dressing gown of his grandfather's with a white frilly blouse beneath borrowed from Mollie Browne, cropped black trousers and the wig which was rather large and half covered his eyes. His hook which he had made with the help of Edward Sutton, looked very fierce.

Sammi stood beside him dressed as Wendy, in a blue tunic topped with puffed sleeves belonging to Toyah, who worked in the Hardy's shop. The little boy who stole the show and won first prize for the younger classes was dressed as Tigger from Winnie the Pooh.

Sammi and Toby were delighted to be given second prize for the older classes. Afterwards, they came rushing across to Shona and Mallory.

'Did you see us?' Toby demanded.

'Certainly did,' Shona told him. 'You were brilliant! Tell you what Toby, I'd better have that wig back. You won't want to stay in that costume for the rest of the afternoon, will you?'

'I s'pose not. OK, come on, Sammi, let's see if we can find Mrs Jones. She'll help us get changed.'

'Are you staying, Shona?' asked Sammi.

'No, I've got to get back because poor Kylie's all on her own in our shop, but Mr Tynedale's going to be around for a bit longer.'

'Only till three o'clock, when Mrs Jennings has got me organised to do a stint on something or other,' Mallory informed them, pulling a face.

'Wet sponges!' Toby giggled. 'I bet it's having wet sponges thrown at you.'

Mallory threw up his hands in mock horror. 'Not the dreaded sponges!'

★ ★ ★

They did a whistle stop tour of the fayre, stopping for a brief chat with Mollie Browne and Kathleen Sutton who were doing a roaring trade on the plant stall. Elaine Jennings appeared by Mallory's side. 'If you're free now, Mallory, perhaps you could come with me. I've got the very job lined up for you!'

'You know what, Elaine, you're a slave-driver!' he said, and Shona saw the slight tinge of pink in the other woman's cheeks, and wondered if she'd got a sense of humour, although how she could work with children and not have one, Shona wasn't quite sure.

Shortly afterwards, she bought some bakes from the refreshment tent to share with Kylie, and made her way back to Jane's Florist.

In her absence, Kylie had taken a late order for a couple of table arrangements and so Shona was very occupied for the last part of the afternoon. She smiled, at the thought of Mallory having wet sponges thrown at him. That she would have liked to have seen!

Shona's mother was happy for her to take Wednesday afternoon off because Shona was going to cover for her the following morning, whilst Kathleen went shopping with one of her church friends. Mallory was waiting for Shona at the studio.

'Now what I'd like to do first of all — if you're agreeable — is to take a few photos of you in various poses, so that I can work from them when you're not available. Is that OK?'

'Yes, of course.'

'Would you mind wearing your hair loose?'

She obligingly untied the ribbon so that her hair tumbled about her shoulders.

'Perfect. You've got such pretty hair!'

To her astonishment he produced a daisy chain and placed it on her head.

'I got the idea when we were judging the children's work. Somehow I thought it was just right for you. You don't mind, do you?'

'Not at all,' she murmured, and he gave her such a brilliant smile that she felt as if she were going weak at the knees.

As he got her to pose for him, moving her arms gently into the right position, he was standing so close to her that she caught her breath, and had a sudden desire to reach out and touch him. Her heart hammered and she willed him to move away.

* * *

After the photograph session, he pulled the easel towards him and, for the next three quarters of an hour, worked practically in silence. Shona hardly dared to move, but was aware that she was getting cramp in her arms. Mallory suddenly noticed her discomfort and looked contrite.

'Sorry, are you getting uncomfortable? I'm afraid I get carried away. Time for a tea-break, I think. I've made a good start and about another half hour will round off this session for today . . . no peeking!'

'As if I'd dare,' she countered.

Over tea, he took out his diary. 'Do you think we can arrange another sitting for next week?' He frowned over an entry in his diary. 'I can't read my own writing! I've written something here against Tuesday — oh, I know — it's the visit!'

'The visit?' she queried.

'Yes, my mother and Miranda are coming so that we can all accompany Gran on a guided tour of The Beeches, and then she's going to stay for lunch to get the feel of the place.'

Shona looked at him in surprise. 'But I thought your grandmother had decided against The Beeches. She didn't seem to like the idea.'

'Well, she's been thinking things over and there are one or two contributory factors now. She's had a chat with her solicitor, Mr Graham, too, although I suppose I shouldn't have told you that. Anyway, it's down to Gran now. She's only going to take a look at The Beeches initially — a return invitation after the tea-party.'

★   ★   ★

During the remainder of the session, Shona tried to get her head round all this. If Mrs Tynedale was seriously thinking about going to The Beeches and having talks with her solicitor — presumably about the financial implications — perhaps, Shona's family ought to be taking matter more seriously too.

'Should we — is there anything my family ought to be thinking about regarding the rose nursery?' Shona asked, as she was preparing to leave the studio.

'How d'you mean?' Mallory's eyebrows arched slightly.

'Well, obviously, if your grandmother's considering selling up, then we need to be prepared.'

He nodded. 'That's why we're having a meeting with Mollie Browne on Friday afternoon. I take it she hasn't told you?'

Shona felt rather ridiculous. Why, she wondered, hadn't her father been invited to be present at this meeting too? Before she had time to say anything further, however, her mobile rang.

'Shona, where are you?' her father asked. 'I've had Adrian on the phone. Apparently, he hasn't got your new mobile number. Anyway, he's coming to see you this evening, so I've asked him to supper.'

'You've done what? Dad!' Shona felt she needed a bit of space after the previous Friday when their dinner date had gone horribly wrong.

'I thought you'd be pleased, love. Anyway, he's leaving work a bit early, so can you get back soon?'

'Problems?' Mallory asked as she finished her call.

'I didn't have when I set out this afternoon,' she told him crossly. 'Now it seems as if they're flying in thick and fast. Anyway, I'd best get back now — we're expecting a visitor. I'll have to let you know about next week.'

'You'll come again then?'

'Of course, why wouldn't I?'

As Shona made to go Mallory blocked her path.

'Wait a minute you've forgotten . . . ' Leaning across he removed the daisies from her hair and then bending, kissed her lightly on the mouth. 'Thank you, Shona,' he said, in such a casual tone, that she wondered if she'd imagined the kiss, but her quickening pulse assured her that she hadn't.

Her father looked up from his newspaper, as she entered the kitchen at the bungalow. 'Shona, I'm sorry if I've put my foot in it. I didn't know where you were and, on the spur of the moment, thought asking Adrian to supper was a good idea. Your mother's made a huge casserole.'

'Yes, I know,' Shona said. 'Not to worry, Dad. It's just that . . . well, there are things Adrian and I need to discuss in private.'

'Have you two fallen out?'

Shona knew there was no point trying to pretend where her father was concerned.

'We had a bit of a difference of opinion of Friday evening — let's leave it at that, Dad. Not having seen each other for so long — well, there's a lot of catching up to do.'

Her father looked at her with understanding. 'Yes, well there would be. I've always liked Adrian. He's bringing his photographs to show us.'

For some inexplicable reason, Shona felt decidedly bad-tempered, as if she had no control over the situation. She was about to mention what Mallory had said regarding Friday's meeting with Mollie Browne, when she noticed how tired her father looked.

Suddenly he seemed to have aged. Remembering how her mother had warned her not to worry him, Shona wondered if that was why Mollie hadn't said anything. Shona laid a hand on her father's arm now.

'You're looking tired, Dad, have you had a bad day?'

'You could say that,' he sighed wearily. 'I was going to wait till your mother came in, but you'll have to know sooner or later. I've had to let young Josh Huggins go.'

Shona gaped at him. 'Let him go! You mean you've sacked him, but why?'

'For a while now, Mollie and myself have had our suspicions that he's been dipping his fingers in the till and, now, I'm afraid we've caught him red-handed.'

'We were a bit busy yesterday morning and left Josh in charge for an hour or so whilst we checked some order. Anyway, a landscape gardener came back this afternoon, for a receipt for a couple of rose bushes he'd bought on behalf of one of his customers. Realised he hadn't got it as soon as he unpacked the roses. Of course, they hadn't been logged — Josh had pocketed the money.'

'I've suspected this sort of thing has been going on for a while now, but couldn't prove anything. Even then, I would have been prepared to let Josh off with a warning, but then Mollie told me she'd had occasion to speak with him previously, because he'd taken a ten pound note she'd left in her kitchen, and although he'd denied it at first, she'd got him to admit it.'

'Did you call the police?' Shona wanted to know.

'No, his mother works for Mrs Tynedale and she's a single parent. He was only on a temporary contract anyway, so it's no big deal as far as he's concerned.'

'Right — we'll have to see if we can find you someone else. There must be any number of students wanting holiday work, or school leavers who'd be interested.'

'It's a bit of a blow. All the same, I desperately need another pair of hands, particularly as the holidays are coming up and there's Toby to entertain.'

Shona wondered what else could go wrong. She set the table and began to prepare some more vegetables.

Adrian arrived at five-thirty. He was carrying a bottle of wine which he gave to Mr Sutton and chocolates for Mrs Sutton. Supper seemed to last for ever as Shona's parents and Toby bombarded Adrian with countless questions about Africa. And then there were the photographs. At nine o'clock Mrs Sutton packed Toby off to bed, despite his protests, and Adrian and Shona went for a stroll along the lane.

'I'm sorry Adrian,' she said.

'Whatever for?'

'Well, you obviously wanted to see me about something and got hijacked by my family.'

He chuckled. 'I like your family, in spite of what I said last Friday, and when your father asked me to supper, I could hardly refuse, could I? Anyway, there'll be plenty of time for us in the future. I wanted to tell you I've been selfish and thoughtless and to make up for it.'

'Right — well, I realise it's going to take us a little while to get to know each other all over again,' Shona told him.

It was a balmy evening and the soft scents of summer were all around them. He took her in his arms and began to kiss her — tenderly at first and then more passionately.

'I've missed you so much, Shona,' he murmured against her hair.

Suddenly images of Mallory came to her and she pulled away from him.

'Perhaps we should take things slowly.'

'It's hardly going to be that fast — with you in Woodhurst and me in London,' he pointed out.

Shona had to smile. 'Well it's considerably nearer than Devon or Africa!'

* * *

They walked back along the lane hand-in-hand, and, although she felt more relaxed, she was aware that the relationship between them was far from being the close one it had been, before he had left for Africa. As they came to the end of the lane, they encountered Mallory walking Juniper.

He called out a pleasant, 'Goodnight.' And then added, 'Next Monday afternoon would suit me fine for that project, if you can manage it.'

'I'll give you a call,' Shona said briskly.

As they walked off, Adrian asked, as she had known he would, 'What was all that about?'

'Oh, just something we're involved in,' she replied impatiently. 'Adrian, for months now we've led our separate lives, so you can't come waltzing back expecting to take up where we left off.'

There was a silence and then he said coolly, 'No, I'm beginning to realise that. At one time there were no secrets between us.'

'It's hardly a secret. Mallory's a neighbour, that's all. He runs an art and craft club at Toby's school.'

'Hmm — well, you certainly haven't wasted any time getting to know one another, have you?'

Shona couldn't think of any suitable reply to that and, shortly afterwards, declining her offer of more coffee, Adrian got into his car and drove away, saying he'd be in touch.

Shona realised then, that one of the things she least liked about Adrian was that he was quite possessive where she was concerned. She could easily have told him about the portrait, but for some reason, had decided against it. She knew she was no longer sure of her feelings for him.

If she cared to admit it, her emotions had been in turmoil since she'd met Mallory.

★ ★ ★

'I thought Adrian would have come in for a coffee before he left,' her mother remarked the following morning, as she

156

refilled the buckets in Jane's Florist with fresh blooms.

'He had to get back,' Shona said and abruptly changed the subject. 'Mum, did you know Mollie's got a meeting with Mrs Tynedale tomorrow morning?'

'Well, of course I did, dear. I just haven't had a chance to fill you in.'

'So, is Dad going to be there?' Shona demanded.

'Well, no, as a matter of fact, but I can assure you he was invited if that's what's bothering you. I would have mentioned it last night, but didn't want to spoil your evening with Adrian.'

'How d'you mean. What's happened?' Shona asked worriedly.

'You're not going to like this, love. Mrs Jennings rang your father yesterday morning and said that in her records Rob names your father as Toby's legal guardian, as of course we'd already told her. Anyway, it seems she's more than happy to discuss any matters relating to Toby's education with your father, during Rob's absence, but not with anyone else.'

'That wretched woman — I hope Dad told her he'd taught for many years.'

Shona began to tidy the stand of gift cards on the counter.

'Not yet, he's keeping that as his trump card. Anyway, no sooner had he made an appointment to see her tomorrow morning, than Mrs Tynedale phoned up saying there was an urgent matter she wished to discuss — only this time Mollie took the call. They arranged the meeting before Mollie realised your father couldn't manage it. Rather than cancel, he thought you could stand in for him, knowing your head for business. That's all right, isn't it, love?'

Shona nodded. 'I guess so. It's all a bit sudden though, don't you think?'

Kathleen Sutton handed Shona some more cards from beneath the counter.

'I just wish it hadn't come to this. Your dad could do without all the stress — that's why he left the teaching profession. He's been looking so tired

158

lately and that Huggins boy hasn't helped matters.'

Shona retrieved a couple of cards she'd dropped on the floor. 'You don't think that's got anything to do with Mrs Tynedale wanting to see us, do you? After all, her housekeeper is Josh's mother.'

Kathleen frowned. 'Shouldn't think so — I have a strong hunch that it's more likely to be what you'd suspected all along, that Mrs Tynedale wants to sell up, and where will that leave us?'

Friday morning came round all too quickly. Shona decided that if this was to be a business meeting then she would look the part and power dress. She donned a neat blue jacket and skirt and swept back her unruly locks in a french pleat.

She was glad she had made the effort for Mrs Tynedale arrived looking frail, but beautifully turned out. Mallory, seeming very business-like, in a dark grey suit, pulled out a chair for his grandmother and then waited until Mollie and Shona were seated round the dining room table before selecting a place next to Mrs Tynedale. Evidently he was attending this meeting too!

'I'm here to represent my family,' Shona told him, catching his questioning gaze.

'My father sends his apologies, but

I'm afraid he's been double-booked. He'd already got another appointment for this morning.'

The meeting started with a brief summary of the accounts prepared by Edward Sutton and read out by Mollie Browne.

'Yes, well that all seems in order — in fact, a few months ago we were only breaking even, but now we're beginning to make a fair profit.' Mrs Tynedale cleared her throat. 'I've every confidence in the way you and Mr Sutton are managing the business, Mollie, however, I have to tell you that, for a while now, I've been considering selling Rose Lodge.'

'Now, I might need to make a decision rather faster than I'd anticipated because, unexpectedly, a property developer has shown an interest in buying the estate. The situation is that it would be the entire estate that he's interested in which would include the land the rose nursery's on and Paddy's Field.'

'I'm just wondering if you'd be prepared to sell up. Of course, I realise that this would be a big decision and that in the absence of Mr Sutton . . . '

Mollie Brown sat as if turned to stone and it was left to Shona to say, 'Actually, my parents jointly own 10% of the nursery, whilst Mollie owns just over 20%, although it doesn't need me to tell you that. So, until both my parents are here, I'm sure you will understand that we can't proceed any further with this meeting. Hopefully, we can reconvene next week. Mollie, have you got the diary to hand?'

Mollie handed it over silently and they all agreed that the following Wednesday morning would be a good time to meet up again.

Shona closed the diary with a snap and looked across at Veronica Tynedale.

'I would just make one comment. Don't be bulldozed into making any decision you might regret later. Now, I'm sure you'd welcome a cup of tea, before you go, Mrs Tynedale. Mollie will look after you ... But, if you'll excuse me, I must return to Jane's Florist.'

Mollie Browne, as if galvanised into action, shot to her feet. 'Come along Mrs Tynedale — into the sitting room. It won't take five minutes to boil that kettle. Perhaps you'd prefer coffee? What about you, Mallory?'

Mallory had got up too. 'If you'd excuse me, Mollie, I'll collect my grandmother in half an hour or so. I've got a couple of things to attend to in the meantime.'

'You knew about this on Wednesday, didn't you?' Shona challenged Mallory, the moment they were outside.

'I can't understand why you're so cross. After all, it isn't strictly any of your business, is it?'

Shona glared at him. 'Then how come you're making it yours?'

He sighed. 'My grandmother asked me to accompany her, otherwise she would have had to have got a taxi. Anyway, I've already explained the terms of the will to you.'

'Yes, you've made it clear that you and your sister stand to gain if your grandmother sells the estate. So obviously you're going to be all for this offer.'

'I thought you didn't want to discuss it,' Mallory said mildly.

'You think yourself so clever, don't

you?' Shona said angrily.

His grey eyes glinted. 'I can't understand why you're so steamed up about it — that's all. Come on — let's turn this on its head, Shona. Have you really considered it from Mollie and your parents' point of view? I don't imagine they're going to want to run the nursery until they're in their dotage, are they?'

'So they might be quite relieved to have it taken off their hands for a fair price. Of course, I suppose you could come into the equation too. Perhaps you're worried about your own inheritance and where you're going to live if you lose Paddy's Field. Is that what's causing you to be so angry?'

'You insensitive, unfeeling brute!' she yelled at him.

Before she realised his intention, he had caught her in his arms and was kissing her firmly on the mouth. For a moment she melted into his arms, feeling as if she were on an emotional roller-coaster, but then she came to her senses and pummelled his chest until he let go of her laughingly.

'It was the only way I could think of to shut you up,' he told her and strolled off in the direction of the gate leading to Rose Lodge, leaving her to shout after him furiously.

'If you ever do that again I'll have you up for assault!'

His laughter rang in her ears and she was incensed. By the time she arrived back at Jane's Florist, she had calmed down, but she still felt upset that Mallory was making a fool out of her, and knew it was because his kiss had disturbed her profoundly. She realised then that it was because she cared about him more than she was prepared to admit!

Shona Pleads Her Case

During Kylie's lunch-break, Shona filled her mother in with what had happened at the meeting.

Mrs Sutton frowned. 'Oh, dear, I do wish your father had been there. You were quite right, of course, to stop the meeting when you realised just what the issues were. With hindsight, we ought to have cancelled it when we realised your father was double-booked. I suppose you haven't found out who these property developers are and what exactly they've got in mind for the land?'

Shona shook her head. 'Anyway, I'm sure all will be revealed at Wednesday's meeting so we'll just have to be patient until then.'

★ ★ ★

'Jenno's done a deal with Granddad,' Toby informed Shona at supper that evening. 'She's gonna tutor me and you're gonna sort out the school garden for her.'

'Toby, I specifically asked you to wait until I'd had a chance to speak with Shona,' Edward Sutton chided him. 'And what's all this Jenno and gonna business?'

Toby bit his lip and Shona said, 'Come on, Dad, what have you let me in for?'

'Oh, Mrs Jennings just wants a bit of help setting up a small woodland garden during the holidays so that the children can plant it up with bulbs next term. She wondered if we could help. She's quite an enterprising lady, I'll give her that and, as Toby says, in exchange she's prepared to give Toby and a group of other youngsters some intensive tuition for a few sessions during the holidays. She's going to rope in a few more parents to lend a hand with the garden. I think she was a bit taken aback when I told her I'd taught for considerably more years than she had! Anyway, I promised we'd support young Toby here, in every way we could.'

The weekend came and, in spite of herself, Shona realised she missed Mallory and that, maybe, she'd made too much of that kiss. She knew she was irrationally upset because it had obviously meant nothing to him.

On Sunday evening, Shona and Toby took Mitzi for a walk. It had been a beautifully warm day. They came across Mallory and Juniper down by the stream.

'Hello, you two. What have you been up to?' Mallory enquired.

'Not a lot,' Toby told him. 'Sammi and Pete are both away this weekend, so I've just been hanging around helping Granddad with a few jobs and things.'

He shot off along the path with the dogs in hot pursuit.

Mallory fell into step with Shona. 'I

know I've blotted my copybook, so far as you're concerned, but is there any chance you could forgive and forget if I ask you very nicely?'

Shona tried to ignore her hammering heartbeat. 'I've promised to sit for you, if that's what you're alluding to, and I don't break my word if I can help it — although, if you don't behave yourself . . . '

'Would you like to bring someone to act as chaperone?'

'Like Elaine Jennings?' she said, before she could prevent herself.

There was a dangerous light in his eyes. 'No, I didn't mean . . . How about tomorrow afternoon?'

'It's a bit short notice. Monday's usually a busy day, but I suppose I might manage to get away around three o'clock.'

Toby came racing back with the dogs. 'Can we go through the woods?' he wanted to know.

Shona shook her head. 'School tomorrow. Let's save it for next week, eh? You're breaking up on Wednesday, so there'll be heaps of time after that.'

Toby looked a bit crestfallen and Mallory noticing suggested. 'Tell you what, Toby, why don't we go along to the inn? We can sit outside with the dogs and you can have a lemonade and some crisps.'

'Just for half an hour,' Shona told him, knowing she ought to refuse.

She rang her mother who reiterated half an hour. It was only a short walk along the tow path to the waterside inn. They chose a table overlooking the river. It was a scene of tranquillity. Shona sipping her drink, wondered again why she found Mallory's presence so disturbing. She watched him now as he chatted away to Toby about football and realised that, in many ways, he was a much easier person to get along with than Adrian, but she had glimpsed hidden depths.

'Felix and Anya are coming to stay in the holidays,' Mallory said now. 'I'm hoping the three of you might be able to spend some time together, Toby. We've got a few things planned.'

'What sort of things?' asked Toby, eyes lighting up.

'Well, we're going in one or two hacks. Perhaps Shona would like to come too.'

Shona saw the excited expression on Toby's face and her heart sank. It was such an expensive thing to do and Rob's quarterly cheque hadn't put in an appearance as yet. She wished Mallory had consulted with her first, but then he obviously didn't have to count the pennies.

'It's a kind offer, Mallory, and I'm sure Toby could spend some time with your niece and nephew, but I'm not too sure what we've got planned ourselves yet.'

Toby's face fell. 'If you're thinking of the work with Jenno,' Toby murmured.

Mallory looked amused. 'What's this?'

'We're helping her with a garden project, aren't we, Toby?' Shona said swiftly, realising he'd blurted this out without thinking. She got to her feet. 'Come on, Toby, time's up. Thanks very much, Mallory. It's been a pleasant little interlude.'

'So,' he said, as they parted company. 'Shall I see you on Monday?'

'You like getting your own way, don't you?' she told him. 'I'll do my best to be there, but sometimes things crop up over which I have no control.'

'Understood, but I'd be eternally grateful,' he told her, a twinkle in his eyes.

Monday morning went by in a flash. There were bouquets to make up for anniversaries, flower arrangements to do in the hotel and the usual floral tributes for two funerals. Shona did not have five minutes to breathe, which was just as well, as she might have backed down from her arrangement with Mallory, if she'd had time to think about it.

Shona worked through her lunch hour so that she could leave early, and hurried back to the caravan to change before making her way to Mallory's studio. When she arrived he was on the phone with his office door open, and she couldn't help overhearing part of his conversation.

'Miranda, I honestly don't know, I've told you, it's difficult to tell with Grandma. She can be very determined. You're just going to have to be patient, it's got to be her decision.' And then after a moment or two. 'I can't tell you that. I appreciate Nathan can't wait for ever! Look, let's just wait and see what happens tomorrow, shall we? I've got to go now, I'm expecting someone. See you soon.'

Shona's mind was racing on. Who was Nathan? And had all this got something to do with the offer by the property developer? She told herself not to jump to conclusions. She called out to Mallory who emerged from his office looking slightly irritated. His expression changed when he saw her. 'Oh good, you've made it! D'you want to see the photos? They've turned out rather well, even if I do say so myself.'

Shona shook her head. 'Surprise me with the finished picture.'

As he worked, she studied him, wondering if he really did have his grandmother's interests at heart. Or if he was more concerned with feathering his own nest.

'You're looking very serious this afternoon, can you relax a little?' Mallory asked, glancing up from his easel.

Shona sighed. 'I've got rather a lot on my mind, that's all. Ever since last Friday my family and I feel as if we've been living under a cloud.'

He raised his eyebrows. 'I can't imagine why. Things can't stay the same for ever.'

'You've no need to tell me that,' she snapped. 'Anyway, we won't give in without a fight.'

'That's the spirit,' he said absently, painting in a few brush-strokes and noticing the heightened colour in her cheeks. She was a remarkably pretty girl and he admired her for supporting her family. He could only hope she would be patient until he'd had the opportunity to sort things out, which could take a little time.

★ ★ ★

'So,' Shona said, as they sat round the table on Wednesday night at what Mollie Browne called a family gathering. 'Have you got to the bottom of what's going on?'

Her father shook his head. 'Not entirely, no. I'll fill you in as best I can. You see, it appears Archie Tynedale wasn't overly concerned about legal documentation regarding his two thirds share in the nursery. When he died his affairs were in a bit of a state. Anyway, the family solicitor has recently retired and the new one is far more astute.'

'Right, so how does that leave us?' she prompted, a trifle impatiently.

Her father sighed. 'Well apparently, as there's no record of a partnership agreement ever having been drawn up, Mrs T can go ahead and sell her two thirds of the rose nursery, if, of course, she can find a suitable buyer.'

Shona tried to get her head round this. She cupped her hands round her coffee mug.

'And now that she's seen The Beeches more fully, what does she feel?'

'She didn't say too much,' Mollie Browne put in, helping herself to a

177

ginger snap. Her solicitor came with her. 'It's my belief she's still not made up her mind and her family are trying to push her into making a decision.'

'Did you find out if the solicitor was called Nathan?' Shona asked, following her own train of thought.

Her mother frowned. 'No, it was strictly, Mr Graham. He was one of those young, know-it-all arrogant types who spoke down to her as people do sometimes with the elderly.'

'That Elaine Jennings does that, haven't you noticed?' Mollie Browne sniffed.

Shona didn't feel they were getting very far. 'Right, so what did you make of it all and what are our options?'

Her father sighed again, wearily. 'Well, I suppose we could find ourselves with a new landlord by the end of the year. Even if we refuse to sell the business to the developers they could still purchase the land and put up the rent and, in all honesty, who on earth is going to want to buy a two thirds share of the business under those circumstances?'

'So you're just going to let them win?' demanded Shona. 'Where's your fighting spirit?'

'It's all very well for you,' Mollie said tartly. 'Young people have got far more get up and go, but this offer Mrs Tynedale's been made must be a good one, or she wouldn't even be considering it.'

There was a silence. Shona looked round at the solemn faces. She for one refused to give up without a struggle.

'OK,' Shona said, 'So if Mrs Tynedale managed to sell her two thirds before the developers stepped in, would that solve the problem?'

Her father drummed his fingers on the table and looked thoughtful.

'They might not be so keen to purchase the rest of the estate without the nursery and Paddy's Field. You see the land would provide good access to the rest of the estate.'

Shona hadn't considered this aspect

and her heart sank.

'So her hand is being forced! She's having to sell her share in the nursery whether she wants to or not, is that it?'

'I think things are getting a little much for her, dear,' her mother said. 'After all, she is in her eighties and she doesn't want the worry of it all, but she will need an income to live on for the rest of her life.'

They were going round in circles and, for the moment, Shona couldn't come up with a solution. 'So what does this Mr Graham advise?'

'He's not a financial adviser,' her father pointed out. 'He was just there to outline the legal implications, should Veronica Tynedale decide to sell up.'

Shona poured herself some more coffee. 'I see. So what do you want, the three of you?' she asked in exasperation.

They looked at each other and her father stroked his chin.

'Well, none of us is getting any younger,' he said. 'I admit, I'd hoped to stay on here at least until I'm sixty-five.

I enjoy the job, even though things haven't turned out quite the way we'd expected due to . . . well, I don't need to spell it out, do I? Come on, Shona, give us your input.'

'Actually, for what it's worth, I also think Mrs Tynedale's being pressurised into this by certain members of her family, as Mollie's already said. There must be other options Mrs T could consider.'

'For instance?' her father prompted.

'Oh, I don't know, but surely there must be some other way!' Shona tore off sheets from her notebook and handed them out. 'Before you make any hasty decisions about selling up, let's list the pros and cons, shall we?'

After a few moments hesitation, they all began scribbling away. The outcome, as Shona had suspected, was over-whelmingly in favour of them keeping the nursery afloat somehow.

'So, what now?' asked Mollie Browne.

Shona smiled at the expectant faces. 'Right, well, I've just had an idea. How would it be if we got a business loan or the promise of one, and went to Mrs Tynedale as a fait accompli offering to buy Paddy's Field and the land the nursery's on outright?'

Kathleen and Mollie Browne seemed lost for words.

'But we can't, we'd never get one,' Edward Sutton objected. 'We've put all our resources into the nursery, Jane's Florist and the bungalow.'

'And regretfully, I haven't a bean,' Mollie added.

'I know that, but what about me? Come on, Dad, you're the mathematician in this family. Come up with a business plan which I can show to the bank.'

'Shona, you'd still need some capital,' he warned.

'And so I have — have you forgotten the legacy from Jane and my little pot of savings?'

Kathleen Sutton looked doubtful. 'Darling, it's a big sacrifice — you've given up so much already and you were talking of putting down a deposit on a little place of your own.'

Shona flung an arm about her mother's shoulders. 'OK, so I can't stay on Paddy's Field indefinitely, but I happen to think it would be a good investment and I'm prepared to try anything to keep the builders away from this patch. If everyone's agreed then perhaps I ought to pop up to see Mrs Tynedale tomorrow — sound her out, before I approach the bank.'

★ ★ ★

Veronica Tynedale looked tired, but she greeted Shona civilly enough. 'I have a suspicion that this isn't purely a social call. Let me guess, you've come to talk to me about the rose nursery, haven't you?'

Over coffee, Mrs Tynedale heard Shona out, listening intently. Shona chose her words carefully. 'You see, I can't help wondering how you really feel about all this. I mean is selling this lovely house and the estate what you really want to do, or are you just trying to come up with a solution that will please your family?'

There was a silence during which Shona wondered if she'd stepped in where angels feared to tread.

But then, Veronica Tynedale spoke. 'You know, dear, you're the first person who's actually asked me that question. Oh, my family have come up with suggestions and asked me what I thought about them, but as to what I really want, deep down, then, no, I haven't discussed that. Probably because it's so personal.'

'Don't say anything if you'd rather not,' Shona said hastily, but Mrs Tynedale smiled.

'No, it'd be a relief. I know that I can no longer manage on my own and that when Mallory goes away, as he will one day, I'll revert to being a sad, lonely old woman again. Things have been a bit complicated in my family of late, and so when I got the offer to sell this house, together with the land, I thought perhaps I'd best go along with it. It seemed a sensible solution to a difficult problem at the time, but now . . . '

'Now you're having second thoughts,' Shona prompted gently.

Mrs Tynedale nodded. 'I keep telling myself not to be selfish, that the young people have got enough to think about without me, but, you know, I love this old house and, if the truth's known, I'd rather spend my last days here than anywhere else in the world.'

'So you didn't like the idea of the residential home or the retirement village?' Shona ventured. Veronica Tynedale settled herself more comfortably in her chair.

'Oh, I suppose they're both all right in their own way, very nice in fact, but all a bit impersonal. Besides, I'd miss my friends and neighbours.'

'The problem is I just can't come up with another answer and, if I can't, what option is there but to sell up and go?'

Shona mulled this over for a moment. 'So what you're saying is that you would really like to stay put, if someone could be found to live here with you — like a companion?'

Mrs Tynedale's blue eyes lit up. 'That's it exactly, in a nutshell. But it would have to be someone I could trust, of course.'

'Well, you know, Mrs Tynedale, I feel sure if you explained all this to your family then they would do their utmost to find someone reliable. I mean there are plenty of agencies that deal with this sort of thing.'

Mrs Tynedale rubbed her hands. 'But, I don't want to raise your hopes, Shona. I'm afraid it wouldn't mean I'd want to hold on to the nursery land and Paddy's Field, even if I didn't sell this house and the rest of the land. You see, there are very good reasons for that. When the end of my life comes, my family will probably sell up anyway, and so the same situation would arise. I would like to feel that the rose nursery and Paddy's Field could be protected in some way from people like Nathan, who just see land as somewhere to build on and line their pockets.'

Light suddenly dawned as Shona registered that Nathan was the property developer. On an impulse, she stretched out and touched the old lady's gnarled hand gently.

'Just remember that whatever you choose to do, is entirely up to you and that no-one else should influence you into making a decision you might later regret.'

Mrs Tynedale smiled. 'You talk a lot of sense, young Shona. Do you know, I feel much happier already, and I think I've just had an idea, but, this time, I'll keep quiet about it until I've had a chance to think it through. If it works out it'll cause a few surprises all round.'

Shona had to smile, even though she was bitterly disappointed that Mrs Tynedale was not prepared to have a change of heart regarding selling her share in the nursery and Paddy's Field.

'You know I almost forgot my other reason for being here, Mrs Tynedale. If you are intent on selling Paddy's Field and the nursery land, to say nothing of your shares, well how would it be if I put in an offer? That's if I can manage to secure a bank loan, of course.'

Mrs Tynedale suddenly became very businesslike. 'I'd need to think about it and let you know, Shona, but you can rest assured that whatever I decide will be in your family's best interests. I don't want to throw Mollie and your father out of the business. I just thought that, like me, they might be glad of an opportunity to retire from it all, especially after all the trauma they've been through recently.'

'That's precisely why they want to continue for a while longer,' Shona explained. 'Who knows, when Rob returns he may decide to settle here in Woodhurst and work in the nursery, after all. The future is a bit uncertain at present, but there's Toby to consider in all of this and he's had enough change in his young life already.'

Veronica Tynedale nodded sympathetically. 'Well, of course, I understand that and I admire you all for what you're doing for the boy.'

'And then, of course, we need to think about the impact on Jane's Florist,' Shona continued. 'We rely on the roses from the nursery. One business tends to complement the other.'

Mrs Tynedale leaned back on her cushions. 'I'm not too sure if Nathan would be prepared to buy the estate without Paddy's Field and the land the nursery's on.'

Shona was determined to clarify something that was puzzling her. 'Is Nathan name of the property developer?'

'Yes, dear. He's Miranda's new boyfriend — no, more than that, her partner.'

Settling Things With Adrian

Shona left Rose Lodge in a daze. Everything slotted into place now. Mrs Tynedale's family would hoodwink her into selling her property to this Nathan, and then he would make a colossal profit. Not only would Miranda get a handout from the sale of the estate the first time round, but if she married Nathan, then she would benefit again. They just couldn't lose, could they?

It had been left that Mrs Tynedale would consider Shona's proposal and let her know her answer the following day.

Shona was so preoccupied with her thoughts that she almost walked past Mallory without noticing him. He caught her arm and she started.

'Hey, why so serious? Were you

looking for me?'

She shook her head. 'I've been to see your grandmother.'

He looked at her intently. 'Oh, what about?'

'As if you didn't know. I think you and your sister are despicable, Mallory!' and she stormed off in the direction of the gate leading to the nursery.

Mallory hared after her. 'Now just a minute, you can't go making accusations like that without any explanation. Just what have you been talking about with my grandmother that's made you so angry?'

'Don't rub salt into the wounds by pretending you don't know,' Shona raged. 'This whole charade is ludicrous. There's been no real discussion and suddenly my family are faced with losing their business.'

'What makes you think it'll amount to that?' he asked gently.

'It's pretty obvious, isn't it? This partner of your sister has made your grandmother some kind of offer for her estate and, whichever way you look at it, your family will benefit whilst mine will be out on their ear.'

'How d'you make that out?'

Eyes blazing she met his gaze. 'If this new brother-in-law in waiting of yours, buys your grandmother's property, then how on earth will the rose nursery survive? Well, I'll tell you one thing, it'll happen over my dead body!'

And shaking off Mallory's restraining arm, she strode off along the path. He whistled, realising that he was going to have to act quickly if his plan was going to succeed.

Toby and Sammi were making a camp at the edge of Paddy's Field. As Shona watched them she felt the anger leaving her.

'Hey you two, come and have some lemonade, and then I've got to get back to work.'

With a whoop, they came rushing over. 'Grandad said it would be all right to be here. Sammi's got her mobile and we're not to go any further than this.'

Shona nodded, realising that they had to have some freedom. Paddy's Field was the ideal place for them to play really, no bigger than an orchard and better than a park in this day and age. She couldn't imagine what would happen if her family had to relinquish the field. Shona could only hope Mallory wouldn't go rushing off to Mrs Tynedale and use his persuasive charm on her, before she'd had a chance to think about Shona's offer.

* * *

Before returning to Jane's Florist, Shona went to have a word with her father.

'So how did it go?' he asked, straightening up from examining some of the stock.

She filled him in. 'Dad, just run by me again how Mrs Tynedale would benefit from selling directly to the developers — apart from the obvious financial gain, of course.'

'That's easy — she wouldn't have to

put it on the open market. It would be practically a private sale . . . Of course, there are strong considerations.'

'What sort of considerations?'

'Well, on the one hand, she'd have some cash in hand but, from the little I know about this sort of sale, she wouldn't get the whole amount in one go. She'd get a certain amount when she signed the contract, but the rest would probably be paid when the development was completed — a kind of safety net for the developers, who, after all, would be taking a gamble.'

He peered intently at one of the rose bushes. 'That doesn't look too happy. Anyway, let's face it, Shona, there is such a thing as planning permission, and that could take for ever, if there were a lot of objections. Of course, I suppose the stipulation could be that Mrs T got to keep the first instalment of the money and that her family would be paid their share on completion.'

Shona picked up a handful of fallen rose petals. 'Hmm, so it's not that straightforward, and the chances are that the builders would pull down Rose Lodge or convert it into something that would bring in more revenue. D'you think there'd be a lot of objection to houses being built there?'

Edward Sutton rubbed his chin. 'I'm not too sure about that. There's certainly a demand for houses in the South East and so if they were the right sort . . . Anyway, we'll just have to wait and see what Veronica Tynedale decides about your offer.'

That evening Shona phoned Adrian. She had a sudden desire to see him, but he seemed a bit hesitant about meeting up, probably remembering their last meeting.

'I've actually got other arrangements for the weekend, but I could manage tomorrow evening,' he told her after a moment or two.

Shona nearly told him not to bother, but thought better of it.

★ ★ ★

Toby had his first lesson with Mrs Jennings on Friday morning and Shona drove him to the school where a group of other youngsters had congregated. She had hoped to have a word with Elaine Jennings about the garden project, but beyond pointing her in the general direction, the headteacher left her to it.

Shona set off to take a look at the designated area. She whipped out her notebook and jotted down a few points. She had a rough idea of what was required and didn't think it would take too long to complete, if she could find some willing helpers.

Toby was rather disgruntled, when she collected him presently.

'School in the holidays is a pain,' he grumbled. 'Dad wouldn't make me go!'

'Your father would tell you the same as the rest of us — that your education is important. You should be grateful to Mrs Jennings for all the extra help she's giving you. It's her holiday too. Tell you what, how about I take you and Sammi swimming this afternoon?'

Toby brightened and Shona dropped him off at the rose nursery and went to relieve her mother at Jane's Florist for a few hours. The phone rang just as she was putting the finishing touches to a bouquet.

'Oh, Shona, it's Veronica Tynedale. Can you spare me a minute or two?'

'Yes, of course, Mrs Tynedale. What can I do for you?'

'I've been thinking about your offer. I hope you don't mind, dear, but I've discussed it with Mallory.'

Shona suspected that she would do that, but hoped he hadn't influenced her decision. To her surprise, Mrs Tynedale continued, 'He thinks it's an excellent idea. After all, if you buy Paddy's field and the land the nursery's on, together with the two thirds of the business, then that will take a lot of the worry from my shoulders.'

'That is, of course, always assuming I can get the business loan.' Shona pointed out gently. She glanced at her watch and frowned. She certainly wouldn't get an appointment at the bank that day. It would have to be for the following week now.

Elaine Jennings appeared in the shop, just as Shona had finished serving a couple of customers with bunches of flowers.

'Good afternoon, Miss Sutton. I'm sorry I couldn't catch up with you this morning. Did you come up with any thoughts about the garden?'

'Yes, I did have a few, but I'm afraid I'll have to tell you about them another time, Mrs Jennings. I've promised to take Toby and Sammi swimming, and I've got one or two things to attend to first.'

'Of course,' Elaine Jennings said pleasantly. 'Perhaps you could wrap up this plant for me? I'm having tea with Mrs Tynedale and Mallory later on.'

Shona wrapped the plant and arranged to see the headteacher about the garden project the following week. Would Mrs Tynedale discuss her plans for Rose Lodge and Shona's offer with Elaine Jennings, she wondered. Surely not!

Kathleen Sutton returned to the shop shortly afterwards, looking flustered. 'I'm afraid Toby won't be going swimming this afternoon, Shona.'

'Why ever not? Is he ill?' Shona asked anxiously.

'No, he's in disgrace! He's broken a window at Mollie's — only he won't own up to it. Apparently, he was kicking a football around before lunch, so it's silly of him to deny it.'

'Oh, no! Do you want me to have a word with him? He's usually a truthful lad.'

'You can try. Mollie's furious, so I've had to bring him back with me. He's sulking outside.'

'I didn't do it,' Toby said adamantly.

'Tell you what,' Shona suggested, seeing that both Toby and her mother were looking fraught. 'How would it be if you came back to the caravan with me for a little while?'

As they walked back towards Paddy's

Field, Toby again said, 'It's not fair! It wasn't me! Pete went home and I just kicked the ball around, but I swear it wasn't near the window. And now Sammi's being punished too, because neither of us can go swimming.'

'Look, it'll all blow over eventually, Toby, but if you did do it, then it's best to own up now.'

'Don't you believe me either?' Toby stormed. 'I wasn't anywhere near the rotten window!' And suddenly, the tears poured down his cheeks. 'I've had a horrible day. First going to Jenno for the extra lesson and now this. I wish my dad was here. He'd believe me!'

Shona put her arms about the small frame and he sniffed into her shoulder.

'Tell you what,' she said presently. 'How do you fancy some ice-cream?'

To Shona's relief, Toby had calmed down by the time she'd fetched the ices, but she continued to be puzzled. If he hadn't smashed the window then, who had?

That evening, Adrian met Shona at the station and they went to a Thai restaurant this time. The food was superb. She considered telling him about the problems at Woodhurst, but decided against it and, instead, listened to what he had to tell her about his job which, up until recently, had been her job.

'I can't imagine why you wanted to leave Hamden's to sell flowers, Shona. You didn't know where you were well off!'

His remark stung her. 'You just don't get it do you, Adrian? In the same way that you love Africa, I love the more simple pace of life in Woodhurst. And floristry isn't just about selling flowers, you know. It's about sharing briefly in people's lives and their happiness, their sadness. You of all people ought to understand where I'm coming from.'

'Hmm,' he said, and was silent for a while, as he sampled the variety of dishes set before them.

'So you've got a busy weekend? Are you working on a project?' she enquired.

'What? Oh, no, as a matter of fact, I've promised to go with Jill to see her parents.'

She stared at him, as his words sank in. 'But they live in Hampshire.'

'That's right. It's her mother's sixtieth birthday, and they're having a bit of a bash so they've asked me along.'

'I see,' she said dully.

Adrian shot her a surprised look, and Shona, trying to be reasonable, added, 'Well, I suppose you've known Jill as long as you've known me.'

He nodded and she thought he looked a bit guilty. 'Jill's got a lot going for her. You, er, don't mind, do you?'

'Mind — no, of course not, why should I?' Of course she did, but she was determined not to let him see it.

Adrian seemed relieved. 'That's OK,

then. Now d'you fancy dessert?'

'What? Oh, no, just a coffee, thanks.'

It suddenly came to Shona, then that she and Adrian had drifted so far apart now that their relationship could never be the same again.

★ ★ ★

They had finished their coffee by nine o'clock and she suddenly made up her mind. Earlier she had thought she might stay at Jill's again but, if she hurried, she could get the train and be back in Woodhurst before eleven. To her relief, Adrian didn't protest but accompanied her back to the station, gave her the briefest of kisses and waved as she went through the barrier.

She rang her parents to let them know she'd be returning that night. Her mother was waiting outside the station in the car.

'Shona, thank goodness you're back!'

'Why? What's happened?' she asked in alarm.

'Nothing bad. Mrs Huggins has been round. She overheard Josh boasting on his mobile to a friend about breaking our window as a means of getting back at us for sacking him. She's at her wits end, poor woman. Apparently, he's been causing mayhem at Rose Lodge and Mrs Huggins is afraid she'll lose her own job. She offered to pay for the window. We naturally refused because we can claim on the insurance, but I suggested Josh might care to apologise to Toby to say sorry.'

'Quite right too. Poor Toby!'

'Yes, I feel dreadful about blaming him, Shona, but what were we to think? Can you take him swimming tomorrow afternoon, and Sammi too, of course?'

'But you're extra busy tomorrow organising the flowers for that big wedding.'

'Oh, we'll manage. We'll just have to get cracking a bit earlier in the morning. I'm more concerned about your father and how he's coping. Josh may not have had much aptitude for the job, but any help is better than no help.'

'And I take it you haven't had any replies to that advert you've put in Sammi's mum's shop?'

'No. I've put one in the window at Jane's Florist now, although I thought the newsagent's was a better bet. It's all such a worry, Shona . . . anyway, enough of that. How was your evening?'

Shona filled her in briefly ending, 'I think there's something going on between Adrian and Jill. They seem to be getting very friendly all of a sudden. They're spending the weekend with Jill's parents who are having a party.'

Her mother said gently, 'You know, much as I like Adrian, I've always had my doubts that he was right for you, love. He's a little too preoccupied with his own plans and, somehow, seems to push yours into the background.'

Shona was forced to agree. 'A year ago I would have been devastated, but now I'm beginning to think the separation was the best thing that could have happened. Imagine if we'd got married and then found we'd made a mistake!'

'I thought you loved him, darling.'

'I thought so too, but if I did, then I've fallen out of love with him, and I always thought absence was supposed to make the heart grow fonder!'

The following morning passed in a flash. As Shona helped her mother decorate the village church for a wedding she realised how much she enjoyed her work. When it was finished, she stood back with a sigh of satisfaction, admiring the effect of the large cream and pink floral arrangements, and the little circlets of rosebuds and variegated ivy at the end of each pew.

A team of ladies had worked tirelessly, polishing the brass and making everything look perfect for the nuptials.

'One day you'll find Mr Right,' her mother whispered, catching her daughter's rather wistful glance. 'It just doesn't happen to be Adrian.'

Shona nodded, and gathering up the rest of the foliage, tidied it away. Back at the shop, they spent an hour making up a number of small orders — a basket of flowers for a new mother, two bouquets for a silver wedding, and several table decorations for a sixtieth birthday party. Kylie was happy to serve in the shop, as she liked chatting to the customers. She then went off happily for an early lunch break.

At around one thirty the door bell rang and Mallory came in. 'My grandmother told me what happened regarding your broken window.'

'Bad news travel fast,' Shona said, sweeping up some flower petals.

'Mrs Huggins was very upset, so she told Gran. Actually, we've had quite a lot of problems with that young man ourselves. We didn't realise until old Harry lost his temper with him yesterday. Josh has been hanging around at the lodge and, although we've attempted to keep him out of mischief, he's been reluctant to pull his weight. It seems he's been selling our strawberries, to say nothing of pilfering from the kitchen. Anyway, his mother's contacted her ex-husband who's in the building trade, and the lad's going to stay with him for a bit.'

'Well, that is good news,' Mrs Sutton said. 'I'm sure Josh isn't a bad lad at heart — just a bit mixed up. Is that why you've called in, Mallory?'

'That, and to ask if Toby would like to come swimming with me this afternoon. I've got a season ticket for that private place attached to the hotel just beyond Woodhurst, and I can take someone with me.'

'I've arranged to take Toby and Sammi to the local leisure centre later on,' Shona told him.

He smiled. 'That's OK, you can all come with me instead. You can have the free ticket and I'm sure I can fix something for the youngsters. The manager's a friend of mine.'

'That's kind of you, Mallory,' Mrs Sutton said swiftly, before Shona had a chance to refuse. 'Why don't I give Sammi's mother a ring whilst you get off to the caravan, Shona.'

Shona opened her mouth to refuse his offer, but then decided she had no good reason to be churlish.

The facilities at the swimming pool Mallory took them to were far superior to those at the local leisure centre.

In spite of her misgivings, Shona found herself enjoying her swim. Who wouldn't in such luxurious surroundings? She couldn't help wondering if Mallory came here to swim with Elaine Jennings. She took a surreptitious glance in his direction, noting the powerful muscles and honeyed tan, and her heart missed a beat. Unfortunately, Mallory caught her gaze and she found herself colouring. Toby was quite a strong swimmer, but Sammi was more cautious and Shona kept a careful eye on her and was grateful when Mallory volunteered to take Toby, first on the diving board and then on the water chute.

Mallory offered to watch out for Sammi and Toby whilst Shona had a turn on the diving board.

Afterwards, Mallory took them into the hotel for afternoon tea. Sammi's eyes rounded as she saw the selection of cakes.

'You must be rich to come in here,' she told him.

Mallory laughed. 'I wish — anyway, enjoy. Everyone is entitled to a treat sometimes.'

'When my dad comes home, I'm going to get him to buy some of those ticket things for here,' Toby said, munching his way through a cream eclair.

Whenever that might be, Shona thought. They were getting a little anxious because they hadn't had so much as an e-mail from Rob recently, although the firm he worked for would surely have contacted them had there been a problem. And, after all, Rob had told his family he would be moving around a fair amount, and wouldn't always be able to keep in touch.

When they had finished their tea, Shona produced some notes.

'My turn,' she told Mallory. 'You've paid for the swims.'

'I've told you it was a cheap round.' He saw the expression on her face and realised how independent she was. 'Look, how about we pay half each? You treat Toby and myself and I'll pay for yours and Sammi's.'

Reluctantly, she agreed and he whisked a ten pound note out of her fingers, although she suspected that it wouldn't cover half, in a place like this.

As they drove away he said to Shona, 'It makes a welcome change to have such appreciative youngsters. I'm afraid Felix and Anya take it all for granted.'

'Well, we can't all come from a privileged background,' she said, and he gave her a sharp glance.

'Ouch,' he grimaced. 'That was a bit of a low blow! None of us can help our backgrounds and perhaps we're not nearly so privileged as you'd like to think.'

He dropped Sammi off at the newsagent's. She looked up at him with large china blue eyes and said, 'Thank you for a brilliant time, Mr Tynedale.'

When Mallory pulled up outside the bungalow, he asked quietly, 'I suppose you wouldn't happen to be free tomorrow evening, or is Adrian taking you out?'

'Actually, I went out with him last night, not that it's any of your business. Do you want me to come for another sitting?'

To her surprise he seemed a bit hesitant. 'No, I was just wondering . . . there are a few things I'd like to discuss with you. Can I take you out for a meal?'

Part of her wanted to refuse, but instead, she found herself agreeing. She knew he would want to talk about her proposed offer to buy Mrs Tynedale's share in the Rose nursery and had been half expecting this.

* * *

Shona spent a long time getting ready for her evening with Mallory. She was fully aware that it was hardly a date, but dressing up made her feel more confident.

When Mallory came to collect her, he raised his eyebrows. She was wearing a simple white dress which showed off her tan. Her hair fell in waves about her shoulders and gold earrings and a chain necklace completed her outfit. He caught the fresh fragrance of her perfume like summer flowers.

For his part, he was extremely good-looking in a light blue jacket and trousers with an impeccable white shirt beneath. He took her arm and she caught her breath.

He drove her to a smart restaurant in the heart of the country where the cuisine was superb. She chose a fish dish whilst he had steak. They were halfway through their main course when he brought up the subject of the nursery.

'This proposal of yours to buy my grandmother's shares in the nursery, together with the land it's on and

Paddy's Field,' he began, giving her a searching look. 'Don't you, er, think perhaps it's a little ambitious, or have you come into a fortune?'

She glared at him. 'I might have known you'd want to pour cold water on it. I suppose you thought I was going to sit back and do nothing?'

He shook his head. 'On the contrary, I can tell you've got spirit. The thing is, without a really good business plan, I'm not sure you'll get too far. After all, the nursery is only making a small profit, so you'd need to prove that you could do a whole lot better.'

She tossed back her hair, hazel eyes sparkling with anger. 'And how do you know what I'm going to propose?'

'Well, obviously I don't, if you're not going to tell me, but I might be able to help. Would you like me to take a look at your business plan before you go to the bank?'

So that was it! For some reason she could not fathom, Mallory was deter- mined to put his spoke in. 'Oh, no you don't! This sale is strictly between my parents, Mollie Browne and your grandmother. You'll get your cut so why are you interfering?'

He raised his hand. 'Hey that's a bit strong, isn't it? I'm on your side, Shona. Whilst my grandmother doesn't want to be bothered with business matters at her age, she's nevertheless going to find it hard to relinquish the nursery, because my grandfather so enjoyed the project.'

She looked at him uncertainly, trying to make sense of what he was saying.

'So part of her still wants to keep her shares in the nursery and the land, in spite of everything?'

He nodded. 'But it just doesn't make sense for her to hang on to it. However, the idea of selling up to Nathan has been worrying her no end, because of the repercussions it might have on your family. I realise she's expressed her concerns to you. I hate to say this, but my mother and Miranda are a bit mercenary. They don't see things the way my father and myself would have done.'

Shona realised it was the first time Mallory had made any mention of his mother. She was a bit puzzled.

'But your mother doesn't stand to inherit any of the estate, does she?'

There was a pause and then he explained, 'She's already received a legacy but, apparently, Gran's also promised her some valuable antiques and china, which she most definitely wouldn't want to cart with her if she moved.'

'I see, and if she decides to stay put — what then?'

'I'm still thinking. Nathan will want an answer from my grandmother shortly. Obviously, he can't wait for ever, but she's not that happy about going into The Beeches. There is, however, one of those rather nice retirement villages about six miles from here. I'm going to take her to have a look next week.'

He took her hand. 'I'm on your side,

Shona,' he told her for a second time. 'Even if it doesn't seem like it at the moment.'

She wasn't sure whether to believe him or not. Perhaps, he was just an accomplished smooth talker.

Shona Realises Her True Feelings

The next day Shona set off for the bank full of hope, to return in low spirits. Her father was serving a customer and she shot past him into Paddy's Field. Presently, she sat outside the caravan toying with a glass of apple juice and staring into space.

'Come back, Miss Sutton,' the bank manager had said, 'when you have a more innovative business plan. I'm sorry to disappoint you on this occasion.'

Suddenly the tears came. Everything seemed so hopeless. A few minutes later, she looked up to see Mallory coming towards her across the field. Her first instinct was to rush inside the caravan.

'Go away,' she told him crossly.

'Aren't I allowed any privacy?'

'I take it things didn't go too well at the bank then?'

'None of your business — just leave me alone!'

He ignored her and perched on one of the plastic garden chairs. 'Come on things are never as bad as they seem. Why don't I make us both some coffee and then you can tell me all about it.'

He disappeared inside, to return a few minutes later with two mugs of instant cappuccino and some chocolate digestives that he'd found in a tin marked cream crackers. 'Not sure about your filing system,' he told her, plonking down the mugs.

'What? Oh!' She gave a watery smile. 'You must think I'm a prize idiot for minding so much — after all, who would want to saddle themselves with a bank loan, anyway?'

'I think you're a warm, caring person, Shona. You and your family have been through a lot in recent years and it's commendable that you want to help them out in this way. Now let me put in my two pennorth, please.'

She was too weary to resist. He helped himself to a biscuit and leant back in the chair.

'I've just had a real heart to heart with Gran. She's confessed that she really hates the idea of going into The Beeches and that, whilst she's still interested in seeing the retirement village, what she'd like to do most of all, would be to stay put.'

He gave her a keen glance. 'But I've a strong suspicion you know this already.'

Shona sipped her coffee. 'I believe she's just been putting on a brave front to please you all.'

'Something like that, but not entirely! She can't manage on her own, any longer, rattling around in that big house. Anyway, if she really wants to stay put, then we're just going to have to see if we can come up with some other solution . . . So, I'm afraid your family might have to be patient for a bit longer and see what transpires.'

Mallory reached for another biscuit. 'Much as I love my mother and sister, they have got their eye to the main chance, and Gran is unlikely to get such a good offer again.'

'So you think they still might try to persuade her?' Shona asked.

'Yes, and, if she can't find anyone to move in with her, then she still might be forced to reconsider. The thing is, Shona, Doreen Huggins has handed in her notice this morning.'

'Why?' she asked blankly. 'If the problems with Josh have been resolved, at least for the time being, then why wouldn't she want to stay?'

'Apparently, she's been seeing someone for a while now and they're going to get married. That's probably what's caused some of the problem with Josh. Anyway, this guy's got his own business and wants Doreen to work with him.'

'Oh, well, I suppose there are a few agencies your grandmother could apply to.'

'We'll just have to wait and see.'

Mallory brushed some crumbs from his T-shirt. 'So, changing the subject, where's young Toby this morning?'

'Round at his friend, Pete's. When are Felix and Anya coming to stay?'

'Next week, so we'll have to find someone to help Gran by then. She's quite capable of cooking, but she's going to need another pair of hands.'

'It seems as if you've got problems as well as us,' Shona sympathised.

They sat in silence for a moment or two and then she said quietly, 'There's something I ought to explain, Mallory. You see, this field is special because it was here that my sister, Jane, first met Rob. She was staying in the caravan one summer with my parents, and he brought them some milk.'

Mallory took her hand between his. 'Memories can be painful, as well as happy, can't they?'

Shona nodded, not trusting herself to speak, and he went on, choosing his words carefully, 'Look, I can't promise anything, so I don't want to raise your hopes just yet, but there is a possibility that there might be a solution to your problem, after all.'

Her heart raced. 'So, aren't you going to even hint at what you've got in mind?'

'I thought you'd tell me again, that it's none of my business. I'll just say that I've been exploring all the options recently and, I'll admit, trying to establish just how much it all meant to you and your family.'

Shona swallowed. 'I'm fully aware that there's no sentiment in business.'

Mallory ignored this remark. His eyes met hers steadily. 'So what does your, er, boyfriend think about all this?'

She was startled. 'Adrian? Well, it's family business, nothing that concerns him. He's been in Africa for over a year and, in comparison with what he saw out there, all this would be small fry.'

'Right — I didn't realise,' Mallory looked thoughtful. 'Leave it to me just for a few days. If I can do something, then I will.'

'Well, that's it then,' her father said, as they ate a hasty lunch together. 'Mind you, it's no more than I'd expected.' He gave a heavy sigh. 'You say Mallory thinks he might have some kind of solution? Did he say what?'

Shona shrugged. 'I'm not holding my breath, Dad. It could be something totally unsuitable.' She got to her feet. 'And now I'd better get back to the shop. At least that seems to be doing OK.'

Shona would have been intrigued could she have heard the telephone conversation between Mallory and his friend that afternoon.

'Have you had any more thoughts about the nursery, Oliver?'

'I'm definitely interested, but I need a bit more time, Mal.'

'Time is what we don't have,' Mallory filled his friend in with what had

225

happened that morning and a few more things besides ending, 'Look, if you are at all interested then I'd advise you to do your utmost to come up with a decision soon, otherwise Miranda and my mother might try to force Grandma's hand. She's so vulnerable at the moment.'

'OK, leave it with me. I'll get back to you, as soon as possible,' came the voice at the other end of the phone.

Mallory came off the phone, whistling to himself. Oliver was an astute business man and, if anyone could turn the rose nursery round and make it come up with a good turnover, then he would be the man. There was no doubt that if Oliver took him up on the suggestion, and everything worked out, then it would set the cat among the pigeons but that was a gamble Mallory was prepared to take.

★ ★ ★

Whilst Toby was having his extra lesson with Elaine Jennings, Shona and a team of helpers that Elaine had somehow encouraged to volunteer, set to work on the new garden. It quickly took shape and Elaine arranged for some gravel and paving slabs to be delivered the following week. Toby seemed a lot happier too and emerged from class with a smile on his face.

'Jenno said I'd worked hard,' he told Shona on his way home. 'She said I just needed a bit of catch-up time.'

'Good, that's what I like to hear.' Shona patted his arm affectionately.

'Mr Tynedale said Felix and Anya are coming to stay at the end of this week. Does that mean I can go riding with them?'

'I don't see why not, but I'm afraid we can't afford it too often.'

'Dad hasn't answered my e-mails. He must be stuck in some weird place away from civilisation, that's what Grandma Browne says anyway.'

'Shona murmured something appropriate, not knowing what to say to Toby. They were all becoming increasingly concerned by the long silence, but as her father had said, no news was good news, so she could only hope he was right.'

Things never came singly, however, and when she got back to the bungalow there was a letter awaiting her from Adrian. She took it into Paddy's Field and read it through twice.

It was brief and to the point. When she had finished, she took a deep breath and wondered why it didn't affect her more. He had written to tell her what she had already suspected, that he felt they no longer had much in common and that, whilst he hoped they'd always remain good friends, he didn't think there was any future for them together any more.

Although it was early days, he and Jill had been out a few times now, and he thought that Shona ought to know before she heard it from someone else.

Perhaps it would hit her later, but, somehow, all Shona could feel, at present, was a sense of relief. When she thought about it, she realised that Jill had always had a soft spot for Adrian.

Shona threw herself into her work, helping her mother with the flower arrangements for the hotel.

'You know, Shona, you've got a real aptitude for this!'

'Must run in the family, mind you I'll never be as good as Jane.'

A shadow flickered momentarily across her mother's face, and then was gone.

'No, dear, perhaps not — Jane had a special gift. Everyone said so, but you have other gifts. I'm sure the garden at the school will be amazing.'

'I'm only doing that because Dad hasn't got the time,' Shona pointed out.

'Oh dear, you do seem down. If you don't mind my asking, is it Adrian?'

Shona sighed. 'I suppose you'll have to know sooner or later, Mum. There is no Adrian. He's dumped me for Jill, and neither of them have had the courage to tell me to my face. Adrian sent me a letter earlier in the week.'

'I know, darling, your father recognised his handwriting. Well, it just wasn't meant to be. As much as I respected Adrian for doing that voluntary work in Africa, I couldn't help wondering if he was putting his own plans before yours, as I've probably told you.'

'Yes, Mum, several times, and I'm sure you're right. Jill and I have been good friends for longer than I can remember. Why couldn't she be upfront with me?'

Her mother flung an arm around her daughter's shoulder. 'Because she obviously didn't know what to say to you.'

Felix and Anya arrived with their father at the end of the week. The first Shona knew of it was when a tall, pleasant-faced young man appeared in the nursery, introduced himself as Oliver Penrose and asked to see Mollie Browne. Mollie was out and it was left to Edward Sutton to speak with him.

Shona was bursting with curiosity, but had to go back to Jane's Florist before Oliver Penrose left.

'What did Mr Penrose want?' she asked that evening.

There was a look on her father's face that she'd seen before when he was keeping things from her. 'Oh, he just wanted to speak with Mollie for old times' sake. He's Miranda Tynedale's ex-husband and has brought the children to stay. Mallory says to tell you, they'll be going on a hack tomorrow afternoon, around two-thirty, and you and Toby are welcome to join them. Can you phone and let him know if there's a problem? Otherwise, he'll pick you up at ten past two.'

She was convinced there was something else. Her father looked pleased about something, but she knew from past experience, it would be hopeless to try to wheedle it out of him until he was ready to tell her.

She was up at six-thirty the following morning, sitting outside enjoying breakfast, when Cimmi suddenly appeared. The little cat very often came to visit and she kept some treats handy, just in case.

'That's my Great Gran's cat!' a voice behind her said accusingly.

Startled, Shona spun round to find little Anya Penrose, standing behind her dressed in spotted pyjamas, fair hair tousled.

'Hello, it's Anya, isn't it? Remember me, Shona? Cimmi and I are good friends. He comes to see me most days.'

The small girl looked about her. 'Do you live in that caravan?'

'Well yes, for the moment. It's quite big inside. Would you like some juice?'

'Yes please, and could I have some toast too? I'm absolutely starving.'

'Anya!' A breathless Mallory suddenly appeared on the scene.

'Oh, hello, Uncle Mal. I'm having breakfast with Shona.'

'So, I see. Mind if I join you?'

'The more the merrier,' Shona said, 'but you'll have to wait whilst I make some more toast.' She suppressed a giggle, because Mallory had obviously been shaving. One side of his face was smooth and the other covered in what might be termed, designer stubble.

Anya burst out laughing. 'You do look funny, Uncle Mal!'

He was totally unabashed. 'Well, what d'you expect? I was in the bathroom when I saw you haring off after Cimmi, so I came after you. You mustn't go out of the grounds like that.'

'I'm not a baby — I'm nearly eight,'

Anya told him, sticking her chin out.

'You'll soon be drawing your old age pension,' he laughed. 'Excuse my apparel, Shona. My grandmother would have a fit, if I appeared at breakfast dressed like this!'

This time Shona couldn't keep her face straight. 'If I'd known it was a pyjama party, I'd have joined in.'

She went into the caravan and chuckled when she peered through the window to see Mallory jogging round the field with Anya in hot pursuit. He was good with children. He'd make a great father.

She emerged from the caravan with a tray bearing a plate of toast and some muffins, and the coffee.

'There's savoury spread, honey and marmalade.'

'What, no strawberry jam?' he asked mischievously.

Anya was concentrating on her muffin.

'This should stave off the hunger pangs until breakfast,' Mallory said.

'Breakfast!' Shona stared at him. 'Are

you telling me you're going back to Rose Lodge for another breakfast?'

'Our official breakfast is at eight o'clock. Porridge and boiled eggs.'

Anya pulled a face. 'Yuk. I hate porridge. Muffins are much nicer.'

'Gran insists on porridge, which she will make herself, and I will attend to the eggs with precision timing. We will forget we've already eaten you out of house and home!'

'Is that why you live in a caravan?' Anya asked, surveying Shona solemnly.

'How d'you mean, Anya?'

'Because someone's eaten you out of house and home.'

When they'd stopped laughing Mallory said, 'You know, Anya, I think you're going to be a comedian when you grow up! Poor Shona we've invaded her quiet time and she's got to go to work soon. Anyway, she's coming riding with us later, aren't you?'

'Certainly am. One thing's puzzling me — you must have left the gate unlocked.'

He inclined his head. 'My fault entirely. I promise to be more careful in future.'

Shona poured more coffee. 'So what's Mrs Tynedale doing about a replacement for Mrs Huggins?'

'She's been asking around, but no luck as yet. Of course, there's our gem of a cleaning lady, otherwise things would be impossible. Anyway, Sylvia puts in a couple of extra hours when she can, and we're all going to have to muck in with preparing the vegetables etc. It's never too early to learn. And — I'll let you into a secret — Mollie Browne has volunteered to cook the roast on Sunday. I remember her roasts from when I was a kid. And her apple pies were sumptuous.'

'Yes, they are pretty special.'

Shortly afterwards they left, Anya clutching Cimmi, and Shona hurriedly cleared the table, changed into her neat trousers and tunic top and rushed out of the caravan. She arrived at Jane's Florist simultaneously with the wholesaler's delivery van.

The morning was incredibly hectic. After running a couple of errands in town for her father, she helped her mother with some flower arrangements for a sixtieth birthday dinner. Fortunately, they were being collected by the customer. Besides that, there were two baskets of flowers for someone who'd recently been in hospital. Shona then held the fort whilst her mother and Kylie went to lunch.

At one o'clock, Mrs Sutton came rushing into the shop looking worried. 'Shona you'll never believe what I've done!'

'Calm down, Mum. Whatever it is, it can't be that serious, surely?'

'But it is! There's that concert at the church this evening and I've clean forgotten I've promised to do the flowers before the rehearsal this afternoon!'

Shona thought quickly. 'Don't worry, I'll phone Mallory and tell him I can't go riding with Toby. He'll understand.'

'You will not!' Kathleen Sutton puckered her brow as she tried to think of a solution.

'I'll just have to leave Kylie in charge that's all and see if Mollie can help me. The two of us together will get it done in time!'

'Well, if you're sure. I'll get back as soon as I can,' Shona promised.

Toby suddenly became rather wary as they approached the stables. 'There's nothing to it,' Felix told him confidently.

Knowing Toby wouldn't want to lose face in front of his new friend, Shona squeezed his arm reassuringly.

'I'll be right behind you,' she whispered. 'If you're not happy, just let me know.'

Shona had been looking forward to spending some time in Mallory's company and was acutely disappointed to find Elaine Jennings waiting for them at the stables.

She was looking trim and attractive in full riding gear. Anya and Felix had the right outfits too and Shona was just grateful that Mallory, like herself and Toby, was clad in jeans and a sweatshirt. Fortunately, the riding school provided hard hats.

Much to Shona's relief, once Toby was mounted on the pony, he began to enjoy the experience. In spite of herself, she could not help but admire the way Mallory and Elaine controlled their horses and, at one point, they went on ahead to canter. Shona was hardly a novice herself, although she hadn't been on a horse for a few years. She kept a close watch on Toby and was pleased to see him relax.

It was a lovely ride along a quiet track by the side of fields of golden stubble, where the corn had recently been harvested. Presently, when they came to a more open area, Mallory offered to stay with Toby so that Shona could have a turn at cantering with Felix, whilst Elaine took Anya for a trot.

'You've been holding out on us,' Mallory said, as Shona turned her horse and rode back towards them. 'I'd no idea you could ride so well.'

'We'd best be getting back now,' Elaine announced in her schoolmarm voice.

'Aye, Aye, Mrs Jennings,' Mallory saluted and she coloured. Shona realised again that the head teacher couldn't take a joke, particularly if it was directed at herself. However, Shona had to concede that Elaine Jennings was extremely good with children.

'That was great!' Toby acknowledged, as he slid down from the pony. 'And I didn't fall off.'

'You were only walking!' Felix pointed out.

'You did very well, Toby,' Elaine praised him, and Shona shot her a grateful glance. 'Now who's coming back to my place for lemonade and cakes?'

'Me!' Anya shouted. 'What sort of cakes have you got, Lainey?'

'You'll have to wait and see,' Elaine told the little girl and, removing her hat, shook free her hair from the restraining net, letting it spell in a dark cloud about her shoulders.

Toby had suddenly gone very quiet, seeing his head teacher in a totally different light and Shona, realising Elaine would probably welcome some quality time with Mallory, said quickly, 'It's kind of you, Mrs Jennings, but I really ought to be getting back. I promised I'd do the last hour or so at the shop, but Toby can stay, if that's OK.'

'I'll drive you back,' Mallory offered, just as Shona realised she'd come in his car.

As if in answer to a prayer, she glimpsed a bus in the distance.

'Thanks, but I'll catch the bus. Toby what are you doing? Make your mind up quickly!'

He opted to stay, and Shona pelted along the road to the stop as the bus approached.

'Do you want this bus or not?' the driver asked testily, as she scrabbled in her pocket, suddenly wondering if she'd got enough money for the fare. Scrambling on, she purchased her ticket and sank thankfully on to the nearest seat, relieved that she hadn't had to go back to Elaine Jennings' house and watch that woman fluttering her eyelashes alluringly at Mallory.

It was then, during that short bus journey into Woodhurst Green, that Shona suddenly realised why she was so uncertain of things. Not only had she fallen out of love with Adrian, but she now found herself more than a little in love with Mallory. It's on the rebound, she told herself sternly. Nothing can come of it, my girl. He's too deeply entrenched with Elaine Jennings!

Relief As Rob Makes Contact

Over supper Toby was full of the events of the afternoon. 'You just wait till I tell Sammi and Pete I've had tea at Jenno's house! You should see the place. It's not a bit how you'd imagine.'

As Shona didn't reply, it was left to her mother to ask, 'What's it like then, dear?'

'All sort of modern — lots of books and CDs, but hardly any things.'

'What do you mean by things?' his grandfather enquired.

'You know things — like you've got on the mantelpiece and in that cupboard over there.'

Kathleen Sutton followed his gaze. 'Do you mean ornaments?'

Toby nodded. 'When we had tea it was done properly, like at Mrs Tynedale's.

Mallory said we can go riding again next week.'

Edward Sutton raised his eyebrows. 'Did he indeed and what happened to Mr Tynedale?'

'Oh, he's on holiday too. Anyway, he said it was all right to call him Mallory because we're next door neighbours. Anya calls Jenno, Lainey.'

'I noticed,' Shona said, 'but you must show some respect, Toby.'

He gave her a mischievous smile, 'Yes, Auntie Shona. Jenno's got some photos of Dad, when he was young, says she'll show me next time.'

'Mrs Jennings has got some photographs of your father? How very strange,' mused Mrs Sutton.

'Perhaps she means in a class photo. After all, schools keep copies over the years, don't they? And Rob did attend Toby's school when he was a child.'

Mrs Sutton's face cleared. 'Of course, now why didn't I think of that, Shona?'

'Jenno was nice to me when Dean, in my class, said my dad's a virtual dad because he's never there. She told him off. All the same I wish he was here. Anya and Felix's dad is coming to see them again on Sunday. It's funny but he has to ask their mum for permission before he sees them.'

'Yes, well, I'm sure it won't be long before you hear from your dad, and he won't have to ask anyone's permission to see you,' Shona told her nephew, gently.

She sincerely hoped Rob would get in touch soon and caught her mother's worried expression.

'Felix and Anya have asked me to go round to play tomorrow. That's OK, isn't it?'

'Yes, dear, but don't go neglecting your other friends, just because you've made some new ones,' his grandmother advised him.

When Toby was in bed Mr Sutton said, 'You know I'm more than a little concerned that we haven't heard from Rob recently. Mollie hasn't heard anything, either.'

'There isn't a great deal we can do, Dad, apart from reassure Toby and sit tight, but, if we haven't heard anything by the middle of next week, I suggest we ring Rob's head office and find out if they know what's going on.'

There was a tight knot in Shona's stomach as she thought about this. Supposing something was wrong and this silence wasn't just Rob's way of getting some space to sort out his head.

Mrs Tynedale came across to Kathleen Sutton and Shona in church on Sunday.

'I'm feeling a bit guilty. I've left Mollie preparing a gigantic lunch for my brood, but she tells me she'll be happy to come to evensong instead. Things seem to be looking up at last. Mrs Stewart over there has just been talking to me and, apparently, her daughter is looking for some temporary work. Karen's training to work in the hotel and catering business, and would be happy to come to help me out during her holidays.'

Shona was longing to ask Mrs Tynedale about the visit to the retirement village, but didn't like to.

It was the middle of the afternoon when Oliver Penrose and Mollie put in an appearance. They were both looking very pleased with themselves about something.

'Veronica's having a rest after Mollie's wonderful lunch, but she's perfectly happy for me to come to see you on my own. I've got some good news for you,' Oliver began. 'Mallory's at the studio with Anya and Felix, if Toby would like to join them.'

Toby didn't need second telling and sped away in the direction of the gate.

Edward Sutton put an arm on his daughter's shoulder. 'You don't mind if Shona listens to what you've got to say, do you, Oliver? She's a valuable part of this enterprise.'

Shona went on ahead to fetch her mother, aware that the others were deep in conversation. Presently, as they all crowded into the sitting room, Shona wondered what she was about to hear.

'Oliver's joining us in the business,' Edward Sutton announced without any preamble. 'He's going to buy Veronica Tynedale's shares, together with the land and Paddy's Field, and then, when we can afford to do, we can buy some of it back from him.'

As her father's words sank in, Shona stared at Oliver Penrose, open-mouthed.

'So you're interested in growing roses?' she asked at length.

'Yes, I always have been, but Miranda wouldn't hear of it. Anyway, when Mallory phoned me up the other week, I thought about it long and hard and realised what a golden opportunity it would be. Of course, I realise I've got a lot to learn, so I hope you'll all be patient.'

'Well, this calls for a celebration!' Mollie Browne said. 'I've got some sparkling wine somewhere, best I can do in the middle of the afternoon.'

Shona still could not believe her ears. At the eleventh hour, Oliver Penrose had stepped in and saved the day and it seemed as if Mallory was somehow responsible.

'So does this mean you'll be moving to Woodhurst in the near future?'

He shook his head. 'I wish, but I'm afraid it's not that straightforward. I wouldn't want to be too far from my children. I'm afraid that, for the time being, I'm viewing the nursery as an investment, but that's not to say I won't be popping in from time to time.'

Oliver got to his feet, saying he'd promised to take the children to see some friends. After he'd gone, Shona's mother turned to her. 'You're very quiet, love.'

'I just hope things are going to work out OK, because from where I'm standing there isn't going to be too much difference in Oliver Penrose owning the land and the shares than Veronica Tynedale.'

'I would have said there was a great

deal of difference,' her father said. 'I'm not sure I follow your argument.'

'I should have thought it was obvious. If Oliver Penrose is only going to be a sleeping partner, then he could decide to sell out if things didn't work out the way he anticipated.'

Her father shrugged. 'We've got to be optimistic, Shona. He's given us some valuable breathing space, time to get our act together and, what's more, you get to keep your capital. I suspect he's had to pay Veronica Tynedale rather more than George paid for it initially and he's prepared to invest in improving the business, too.'

'Oliver's divorce and settlement to Miranda were already finalised when his father died recently. Anyway, he's inherited some capital which he wants to invest. He happens to believe in us. Mollie knows him quite well and has every confidence in him, don't you, Mollie? So, you see, we're all happy with the arrangement — so why can't you be?'

Shona could not put into words what she felt. Without another word she went off to the caravan, just as Mallory and Toby came into the nursery.

'Felix and Anya's dad is taking them out so I've come back,' Toby informed her. 'Where's Granddad?'

As Toby shot off to find Edward Sutton, Mallory said, 'He gets on really well with Felix and Anya. I've arranged for both of them to go riding again at the end of next week and Toby's welcome to join them.'

'You're good at that, aren't you, Mallory — arranging things,' she said tight-lipped.

He stared at her, sensing the barely suppressed anger, and clueless as to what he had done to upset her now. 'Are you going to tell me what I've done wrong?'

He followed her into Paddy's Field and, as she rummaged in her pocket for the key to the caravan, put a restraining hand on her arm. 'Please, Shona, how else can I put things right?'

She sank down at the table. 'You put the idea into Oliver Penrose's head about buying your grandmother's share of the business and the land. You knew how keen he was — yet you let me go ahead with seeing the bank manager. All this time, you must have been laughing up your sleeve.'

'How d'you make that out?' Mallory looked genuinely puzzled. 'I thought you'd be pleased that I'd managed to come up with a solution to your problem, but I didn't know if it'd come to anything.'

She glared at him. 'Hadn't it occurred to you, Mallory, that I wanted to solve the problem on my own? It's oh so easy for people with pots of money to invest in whatever they choose, but to do something through sheer hard graft, to work up from the bottom and achieve a result, that's quite different.'

'Aren't your parents pleased?' he asked, feeling at rather a loss.

'Oh, they're over the moon, but they

can't see beyond the next year or two. What happens if Mrs Tynedale decides to sell the remainder of her estate to Nathan and, in a year or two's time, Oliver grows tired of the nursery and decides to sell out again — only this time to him as well? Where would that leave us?'

'It won't happen — you can rest assured on that score. You see Oliver isn't like Miranda. He doesn't have a grasping streak.'

She stared at him in disbelief. 'But he's recovering from a divorce, so if he's got the opportunity to put one over on Miranda then . . .'

Mallory gave a short laugh. 'Oliver isn't like that, Shona. He wouldn't seek revenge.'

'Let's hope you're right. Anyway, just now our most immediate priority is to find someone to replace Josh, and to stop my father working himself into the ground.'

'Oh that's easily sorted. Actually, it's your father I came to see. That young girl, Karen Stewart, who's coming to help out at Rose Lodge had just called to see us. It seems she's got a boyfriend who's also looking for some casual work. When I mentioned the job at the nursery, she thought it would suit him fine. I told her to get him to get in touch with your father, but thought I ought to have a word with Mr Sutton first.'

She gave him a cold look. 'I'd have thought you'd have done that in the first place. And, is this friend of Karen's trained to do nursery work?'

'Well, no, but he did do some work experience in a garden centre, apparently, and Gran knows him and says he's a very willing lad.'

'So that's all right then!' Shona knew she was being churlish. 'My father's possibly still in the house or he could be in one of the greenhouses. And now, if you'll excuse me, I've got a few things to do.'

Mallory watched Shona as she climbed the steps to the caravan and inserted the key. He could have cursed himself for being so insensitive. She was a very independent young woman and, somehow, he had managed to upset her feelings.

Inside the caravan, Shona sat on her bed trying to analyse why she felt so angry with Mallory. She realised it was because she was feeling shut out. She knew she was being unreasonable, but she couldn't help herself. She had given up a good job to come here to Woodhurst and willingly, but now it was as if her opinion didn't count. Life had changed suddenly and dramatically for her family, when Jane had died on that fateful day in the Cairngorms.

Shona had believed she was serving some purpose by coming to Woodhurst, but suddenly, it seemed she wasn't. They were all managing perfectly well without her input. She pressed her hands to her forehead. What was she to do? She couldn't easily return to Hamden's because Adrian had filled the post that had once been hers

— even, if only on a temporary basis. Anyway, she wasn't sure how she'd feel about being there now. No, she was going to have to think long and hard about her future.

Shona's thoughts turned to Veronica Tynedale. Would she still sell Rose Lodge and the rest of her estate to Nathan or would she carry on living in that big old house for a bit longer? And then there was Rob. Was he so engrossed in his new work abroad that he'd put his family out of his mind?

A sudden blaze of anger filled her. He had no business neglecting his young son and Mallory and his family should be considering what Veronica Tynedale really wanted and putting her needs before any schemes of their own.

She sighed. For a short time she'd allowed her heart to be taken over by a suave young man. Well, she'd come to her senses just in time!

Shona went across to the house feeling the need for company. The nursery was closed for the day and her parents had gone home. Mollie Browne was sitting at the kitchen table staring into space and looking upset.

'Mollie, whatever's wrong?'

'Oh, I'm just being daft — thinking over old times and how things used to be, but you see it's the end of an era for me.'

Shona put the kettle on and sat down beside the older woman. 'I'm sure we could all wish we could turn the clock back, Mollie. Come on, tell me what's sparked all this off?'

Mollie sniffed, 'Going up to Rose Lodge just now. I remembered how things used to be when George and I worked there. We had such good times.'

'But I thought you found Mrs Tynedale a bit overbearing.'

'Oh, she's all right when you get to know her. I feel so sorry for her at the moment. The upshot of it is that she really doesn't want to leave Rose Lodge. She's being manipulated by that daughter-in-law and granddaughter of hers, you mark my words.'

'Mollie, there really isn't anything else we can do because, at the end of the day it isn't our business,' Shona found herself saying.

'You don't believe that, do you, Shona? If you did you wouldn't have made such a stand about retaining the nursery.'

'I guess you're right. Got any suggestions?' Shona asked and got up to make the tea.

'Well, yes as a matter of fact I have. I've been having a long hard think this afternoon. Oliver hasn't signed any agreements yet, has he?'

Shona shook her head. 'Hardly. There hasn't been time for any documents to be drawn up. After all this time, things must be done more — more . . . ' she stopped, trying to be diplomatic. Mollie Browne poured the tea and then reached for the cake tin. Shona waited, wondering what the older woman was about to say.

'Going up to Rose Lodge today made

me realise that, since George has died, I've not really been happy working at the nursery. It was never my forte. I love the roses, don't get me wrong, but my heart's just not in it any more. It was George's thing not mine. George and Archie Tynedale had a real feel for roses, the same as your father, but for me, it's arranging them. I enjoy doing that, but just as a hobby.'

'Do you mean you'd be happier working in the shop, Mollie? Because, if so, then I'm sure I could swap with you periodically,' Shona prompted, realising that it wasn't exactly what she'd had in mind when she'd offered to help out and, momentarily, forgetting her resolution to leave Woodhurst.

Mollie sipped her tea, deep in thought. 'No, dear. What I'd really like to do is to go back to Rose Lodge, so that Veronica Tynedale can keep her independence. Now, before you say anything, please hear me out.'

Shona was incapable of speech for a few moments, anyway. Mollie was older than her mother and it would be a big undertaking.

She selected a piece of cherry cake. 'D'you mean as a companion?'

'No, of course not! I'd do the cooking like Mrs Huggins did, arrange the flowers and be a housekeeper. The work wouldn't be any harder than it is at the rose nursery.'

Shona was silent, thinking that she couldn't actually see how that would solve anything. It would certainly only serve to create even more problems for the rose nursery, as they'd be without another experienced worker.

'Shona, I can see you're not happy about this. Probably, I should have spoken with your parents first. There are a number of things I can't tell you at the moment, because it's all a bit complicated, so you'll just have to trust me. Now, can we please the change the subject?'

'OK, but just tell me one thing. Does this mean you'll want to sell your shares in the nursery too?'

But Mollie Browne refused to be drawn on this one.

Shona's head was in a whirl. Of course, she wanted the best for everyone, but it seemed as if they'd come back to square one.

She sat staring into her teacup wondering if she'd made a colossal mistake in coming to live in Woodhurst. She wanted to ask so many questions, but could see from the set expression on Mollie Browne's face that, that lady wasn't going to commit herself, and was probably regretting having said as much as she had.

Shona couldn't imagine how her parents would cope with the news. At present, they seemed to be receiving blow upon blow. She said, 'You've asked me to change the subject and I've just thought of something I've been meaning to ask you. Toby mentioned some photographs Mrs Jennings said she'd show him of his father, and I was just wondering what they might be.'

Mollie Browne brightened visibly.

'Oh, now that's easy. You see, years ago when George and I worked at Rose Lodge and Mallory and Miranda came for their holidays — well Rob used to hang out with them — if that's the right expression. Anyway, Elaine Jennings, or Peters as she was in those days, came to stay too. She was one of these clever, scholarship girls and was a school friend of Miranda's — a bit older than Mallory. She was always ambitious, but came from quite a poor background.'

'Anyway, there was a time when she and Rob — well they went out for a while. In fact, if it hadn't been for her filling his head with grandiose ideas then maybe Rob would have been content to have helped his father in the rose nursery, but she encouraged him to better himself and train as an engineer.'

'But surely it isn't a bad thing — motivation.' Shona interrupted.

Mollie frowned. 'That one's too ambitious for her own good. No time for people who aren't useful to her either. Anyway, they all went off to university but still met up in the holidays. Elaine never thought my Rob was good enough for her and ended up marrying a man almost old enough to be her father, but very wealthy. At the time, Rob was heartbroken but, personally, I think he made a lucky escape. Of course, it didn't work out but, by then, Rob had met Jane and, believe you me, Shona, she was the love of his life — such a lovely girl. They were both so happy. It was so unjust that what should have been a lovely holiday ended so tragically . . . ' her voice broke and Shona felt her own eyes filling.

She touched Mollie's hand gently. 'We must just be thankful that Toby wasn't there.'

They sat in silence for a few moments and then Shona asked, 'So Elaine Jennings and her husband got divorced?'

'No, they were separated when he died, so she inherited most of his considerable estate. She doesn't need to work, I'll give her her due there. She's good with children, I'll grant her that too. And now that Mallory's back in Woodhurst — well, who knows.'

Shona tried not to think about Elaine and Mallory. It hurt too much.

'Well, I hope the photographs won't upset Toby. I mean if they're of her and Rob . . . '

Mollie Browne shook her head. 'She might not be my most favourite individual, but she would never do anything to upset a child. I expect they're just group snapshots. I just wish Rob would get in touch. There are things I need to discuss with him.'

Shona returned to the caravan with a heavy heart. The future seemed bleak for her family and she wondered how things were going to work out.

Brett turned up the very next morning, a fresh-faced young man with a shock of red hair. Apparently, he had completed a science degree and been on a gap year and now he was casting around for some suitable work. By lunchtime, Edward Sutton had realised his potential. He was a good worker and quick to learn. For the first time in ages, Edward began to feel as if things were looking up, at least as far as the nursery was concerned.

Shona was about to return to Jane's Florist after her lunch break, when Mallory appeared waving some mail.

'Karen found these stuffed behind the back of some jars in the pantry.

Harry tells me he remembers the postman handing him some mail when Josh was around. It seems Harry asked Josh to take it up to Rose Lodge but obviously he decided to ditch it! Judging from the postmarks, it must have been a while back. I'm sorry, Shona, some of yours is mixed up in it — it looks as if Josh was asked to deliver that as well!'

With a hammering heart, Shona practically snatched the mail from him and sorted through it. Amongst the invoices were two postcards from Rob.

'Thank heavens for that! We've all been so worried about Rob. I can't begin to tell you!'

She scanned the postcards. 'Seems he's had a few days leave before beginning a new phase of his work. He's been in an isolated area and says he hopes we received his last e-mail.' She shook her head. 'What e-mail? We've checked every day. Mallory, you don't suppose Josh could have deleted it? No, surely even he couldn't stoop that low!'

Mallory frowned. 'Let's hope not, but I suppose we'll never know, anyway at least you know Rob's OK, so that must be a relief for you.'

Shona beamed at him and, on an impulse, threw her arms round his neck and planted a kiss on his cheek. 'Certainly is. You can't begin to imagine. Thank you so much, Mallory, for bringing this over. Toby will be ecstatic!'

Suddenly she became aware of the way he was looking at her and, cheeks flaming, pulled away. 'I'm so sorry. I don't know what came over me.'

Before she knew what he was about, he had caught her in his arms and was kissing her with an intensity that made her breathless. Her heart beat wildly.

'Well, Miss Sutton, that really was a very nice thank you! I must bring over your mail more often.'

'Don't push your luck,' she told him, trying to get a grip on herself. 'Now I'm due back at Jane's Florist shortly, so if you don't mind . . . '

'Not at all,' he told her pleasantly, as if they'd just been discussing the economy. 'Of course, I was hoping to persuade you to come for another sitting for your portrait. It's looking good.'

'I'm afraid I'm busy for the rest of the day,' she told him lightly. 'Anyway, I thought you were supposed to be looking after Anya and Felix.'

'Oh, I didn't mean today. Elaine's coming over and we're all going swimming. No, I meant Wednesday afternoon, after Oliver's meeting with Mollie and your parents.'

'I see,' she said dully, again feeling sidelined. As usual, she'd read too much into the situation. It was her fault. She ought never to have encouraged him.

'Well?' he asked, head on one side, watching her.

'Well, what?' she asked testily.

He sighed. 'Will you come to sit for

me on Wednesday afternoon, about fourish when Oliver takes the children out? I'll promise to be on my very best behaviour,' he added with a twinkle in his eyes.

Before she could reply, Anya shouted to them from the edge of the field.

'Lainey's here! We're all waiting for you, Uncle Mal.'

Elaine Jennings came to stand beside Anya. She was dressed in a red shirt and black trousers, her glossy dark hair tied back neatly with a velvet ribbon, her make-up impeccable.

Shona, aware of her own rather dishevelled appearance, realised that there was simply no contest where the other woman was concerned.

Mallory regarded Shona merely as a model for his painting, and she was aware that she didn't like it — not one bit. But then he wasn't to know that her emotions were in turmoil and he was responsible!

Toby and the rest of the family were ecstatic that they'd heard from Rob, although the thought that Josh could have behaved so badly, was rather disturbing.

'It would be even better if Dad came home,' Toby said that night over supper. 'Anya and Felix's dad's coming to take them out on Wednesday afternoon.'

'Well, we'll have to go out somewhere too, won't we? How about a picnic, and you can ask Sammi and Pete?'

Toby brightened and then looked crestfallen again as Kathleen Sutton said, 'Not on Wednesday, love . . . You've got to go to the dentist with Grandma Browne.'

'I can take him,' Shona put in quickly. 'If Oliver Penrose is coming to see you all, you won't be able to spare her.'

'Mollie has an appointment too, but it's not until the afternoon and we should be done by lunchtime.'

If Shona had thought she had a ready made excuse to back out of her arrangement with Mallory, she realised she was mistaken. She wondered if Mollie Browne had spoken to her parents yet about wanting to give up working at the nursery, and knew she couldn't really broach the subject herself, without dropping Mollie in it.

On Tuesday, Shona took Toby for his extra literacy class and then went off to do some work in the garden. To her surprise Mallory was already there, dressed in jeans and T-shirt. He grinned at her and indicated some bags of gravel.

'Elaine's a bit short of volunteers this morning so she's roped me in to lend a hand. And now a couple of others have pulled out at the last minute, so it looks like it's just you and me.'

And Elaine was not going to like that one bit, was she? Especially, as she wasn't free to supervise. However, no sooner had Shona had this thought, than Elaine appeared.

'My deputy head's in this morning, so I've left her in charge for a short while. My secretary tells me we don't have any other volunteers this morning, after all, so if you want to leave it for another day?'

'We're here now, Elaine,' Mallory pointed out, 'and I'm sure I can carry a few bags of gravel, if Shona cares to tell me what she wants doing with them.'

If looks could have killed, Shona thought she would probably have expired on the spot, but, after a moment or two, Elaine Jennings said pleasantly, 'Well, I'll leave you to it then and get back to my charges.'

For a while they became business-like, and worked like Trojans to get the gravel beds filled. The garden was taking shape and looking very attractive. Here and there Shona had left spaces between the paving stones, to be planted with bulbs by the children.

'You've got an eye for this,' Mallory said, as he looked around him.

'It used to be my job,' she told him, 'although I rarely got the opportunity to be hands on.'

He smiled. 'Well, you're obviously in the fashion.'

'How d'you mean?'

'Multi-skilled. They tell me that's what every employer is looking for these days.'

'Good. Although I don't think I'll be changing my job for quite some while yet, but I'll bear it in mind when I do.'

She stood back hands on hips to examine her work.

'Actually, I'd welcome some input, Mallory. What d'you reckon to this?'

'You've done a great job. I couldn't have done it better myself!' he teased, looking at the neat slate beds and zig-zag path.

She realised, with a lump in her throat, that her feelings for this man were far from that of a friend. She was so conscious of him standing there beside her — of his sheer masculinity and the fresh clean fragrance of his cologne. There was a magnetism between them that was tangible. The moment was broken by Toby rushing into the garden.

'Jenno says you can come for coffee? We're having lemonade in the dining room.'

Mallory looked amused. 'That's an offer I can't refuse. Tell Jenno we'll be right there.'

Toby stopped, cheeks red. 'Oh, I mean Mrs Jennings. You won't tell her, will you?'

'Scouts honour!' Toby scuttled off and Mallory chuckled.

'He's a character, your nephew. Tell me, what is it he does with Elaine?'

'You mean she hasn't told you?' Shona was frankly surprised.

'Elaine is as close as the grave when it comes to professional matters, believe you me, Shona. She might have her faults, same as the rest of us, but telling tales out of school isn't one of them, if you'll pardon the pun.'

It was Shona's turn to colour. 'Of course, I'm sorry, I didn't mean . . . Promise you won't let on I've told you.' She explained briefly about the additional literacy.

Mallory looked sympathetic. 'Poor kid, I suspected it might be something like that. He's had such a rough time of it, but Elaine's very good.'

Shona was forced to agree. It seemed Elaine Jennings was wonderful at everything, including landing herself Mallory as a boyfriend.

'Of course, my father is a bit out of

touch with modern literacy methods, but he's perfectly capable of working with Toby and carrying on Mrs Jennings' good work. As I've told you before, he used to teach maths and got excellent exam results.'

'He's obviously multi-skilled too!'

'Yes, and that'll come in handy if the business fails, won't it?' Shona said rather tartly.

'The Two Of You Are Made For Each Other'

Soon after Toby and Shona arrived back at the bungalow on Tuesday lunchtime, Edward Sutton called the boy into the office. A few moments later he came rushing out waving a piece of paper.

'Shona! Shona! My dad's sent me an e-mail. He's had a bit of trouble getting on the internet. Guess what! He's coming home around my half-term in October and he's going to take me on holiday!'

Shona hugged the boy to her, relieved that things were at last looking up for him.

When her father handed her a letter from London, however, she took it to the caravan and read it as she ate her lunch. It was from Jill, telling her that she and Adrian were engaged. They were going to get married soon after Christmas and then going to Africa. Jill ended by saying she hoped there would be no hard feelings. Shona supposed she ought to have been more upset but, apart from being slightly peeved that Adrian hadn't written to tell her himself, felt quite unemotional.

Shona was fully occupied on Wednesday morning. The shop seemed busier than ever.

Much to his disgust, Toby had been set to work on his literacy homework which was a piece of creative writing.

'I'm not going to see Jenno again until next week,' he complained.

'I know but once it's done, it's done — anyway, I thought you were going riding later this week. And there's the picnic to look forward to.'

Toby looked sullen. 'It's not the same as going to the seaside or a theme park.'

Shona sighed. 'I'll try and see what I can come up with, but I'm not promising anything.'

An hour later she took him with her to do the deliveries and he brightened up when he encountered one of his young friends, whose mother invited him to join them on an excursion to go skate-boarding in the local park.

The meeting with Oliver Penrose over-ran, making Mrs Sutton late back to Jane's Florist. Shona sent Kylie off for her lunch-break and had just finished serving a customer when her mother rushed in looking harassed, and turned the shop sign to closed.

'Shona, why ever didn't you tell me what Mollie Browne had in mind? She said she'd mentioned it to you. Your father and I are both shell-shocked. Some warning would have been nice.'

Shona swallowed. 'When Mollie spoke to me, she was still mulling things over. I didn't want to tell you because I didn't want to worry you unnecessarily. As it is, I still don't know what she's decided.'

Shona and her mother went into the small back room and sat amongst the flower arrangements, drinking cups of tea.

'Mollie's decided to quit working at the rose nursery and go up to Rose Lodge, but not until Karen goes back to university. For the time being, Mollie's going to hang on to her share of the business until she's had an opportunity to discuss things with Rob. There's so much going on my head's spinning!'

As Mrs Sutton sipped her tea, Shona wondered what other revelations she was about to hear.

'But Oliver Penrose is still going to buy the land and Mrs Tynedale's shares, isn't he?'

'Oh yes, he hasn't rescinded on that, thank goodness. It's just that, well, to be frank, I'm finding it hard to credit what Mollie's decided. Apparently, Mrs Tynedale approached her on Sunday, told her there was an opening for her back at the lodge, but that she wouldn't pressurise her into making a decision until she'd had a chance to think things over . . . and that's not all.'

'Surely there can't be more!' Shona stared at her mother.

'Oh, but there is. Since Oliver's mother has been widowed, she's finding it difficult to adjust to living on her own. After Miranda and Nathan are married, they intend to move and so Marian Penrose won't be so involved with her grandchildren. Mrs Tynedale gets on well with her and has asked her to consider living at Rose Lodge, as her companion, and Marian has agreed — although it won't be quite yet because of the wedding. In the meantime, Veronica Tynedale has decided to employ someone from an agency, on a temporary basis, to help her out.'

Shona's brain had gone into overdrive. 'So where does that leave us?' she wanted to know.

Her mother sighed. 'Your father's all for putting an ad in the paper straight away for another experienced worker, but Oliver and Mollie have persuaded him to leave things as they are for the time-being.'

'And what do you think?'

Kathleen Sutton looked surprised. 'Me? Well, I'll naturally support your father in whatever he decides to do.'

'That wasn't actually what I asked, Mum,' Shona pointed out gently.

'Well, I haven't had a proper chance to speak with your father yet, but I actually go along with the others on this one. It's no good rushing into things. We've got to see what transpires. Young Brett's a keen worker and has expressed an interest in learning the business, and as for Oliver . . . well, we'll just have to wait and see, won't we? I did hear a rumour that . . . ' she trailed off abruptly leaving Shona none the wiser. 'And now we'd better open up. Time is money. And, before you ask, no, I haven't forgotten that you're off on some mysterious assignation of your own at four o'clock. All I ask, Shona, is that you don't go dreaming up any more schemes — at least for the time being!'

That afternoon Mallory allowed Shona to look at the portrait. 'There, what d'you think?' he asked, watching her face intently, as she studied the painting. She knew it was a good likeness. To her surprise, he had captured her in a pensive mood and she was stunned to see that he'd set her portrait against the backdrop of Paddy's Field.

His expression was serious as he surveyed her. 'You don't like it!'

'Yes — yes, of course I do,' she assured him. 'It's just different from how I expected that's all.' Her lips curved in a smile. 'Actually, I love it! You're really talented, Mallory and I'm privileged to have been your model.'

He took her arm. 'With your permission I'm going to call it 'Flower Girl', because that's how I see you. Now, there are just a few more finishing touches to do.'

For a few moments he worked in silence and she watched him, aware that she'd be sorry when all this was over and there was no longer an excuse for her to see him at the studio.

He looked up and eased his back. 'Well, you ought to be feeling pleased with yourself,' he commented as he studied his painting critically.

'How d'you make that out?' Shona asked him, settling in a more comfortable position.

He wiped his brush. 'You've managed to achieve a result which none of the rest of us have managed to do.' Seeing Shona's puzzled expression he added, 'With my grandmother. Oh, I'm aware of the little chat you had with her, and it's helped her to make up her mind about her future.'

'Oh,' Shona managed lamely, wondering if he was about to throw his paint palette at her.

'Come on, Shona, I can't paint you with your eyes closed — at least I don't want to.'

Her expressive hazel eyes flew open. 'Are you very angry?'

For an answer, he set down his brush and came across to her in a purposeful manner, so that she caught her breath. 'Do I look angry?'

She shook her head. 'But, you've every reason to be, I mean Nathan is going to be your brother-in-law and Oliver's your friend and . . . '

'Once before I told you that the only way I could stop your chattering was to do this . . . '

He caught her in a tight embrace, and then his lips met hers in a long tender kiss that sent her senses reeling and her pulse racing.

'There!' he said at last. 'It works every time. Shona, you really are the most amazing girl I know.'

He had, as he had predicted, rendered her speechless but, then she managed to murmur, 'Oh, what makes you say that?'

'You're really not thinking about yourself in all of this, are you? You've just been quite selfless, intent on sorting out everyone else's problems and helping an old lady to make up her mind about where she wants to spend the rest of her life.'

She swallowed. 'I've interfered, you mean.'

Mallory looked at her affectionately. 'Maybe, but with the best possible motive. When the dust settles, I'm sure everyone will see that it was all for the best.'

'So what about Paddy's Field? Do you think Oliver will want to build on that? And what about Mrs Browne's share of the business?'

'Stop!' he commanded. And this time he placed a finger gently on her lips.

'It'll all work out, Shona, believe you me. Don't you think it's about time you gave some thought as to what you want for yourself?'

She smiled at him unsteadily, aware that she knew only too well what she wanted for herself. She had known for a while now, ever since Mallory had walked into Jane's Florist on Veronica Tynedale's birthday, but it was all so hopeless.

He caught her hands between his. 'I've thought long and hard about the best way of doing this — a romantic, candlelit dinner in an expensive restaurant, a moonlit walk along the river bank or a dozen red roses, but when it comes down to it, I . . . '

'Mallory, what are you talking about?' she asked wonderingly.

'Well, it's like this . . . I've fallen in love with you, my beautiful flower girl, so do you think, I mean, is there any possibility that . . . '

This time it was Shona who silenced him with a kiss.

As she lay in the shelter of his arms, she asked, 'What about Elaine?'

His eyes widened in incredulity. 'Elaine? Shona, Elaine and I are good friends — nothing more. She's like an older sister, fiercely protective if she thinks I might get hurt. You see, I did once a long time ago — a brief engagement to a rather self-centred girl, but, since then there's never been anyone else that I've felt serious about. Anyway, it's my belief that, given time, Elaine and Oliver might just happen to . . .'

She looked at him incredulously. 'I didn't realise, I'd never have guessed . . .'

'Ah well, there you are then — and what about Adrian?'

'Adrian is returning to Africa after Christmas and my ex-flatmate and friend, Jill, is going with him. I heard from her yesterday morning. They're planning to marry before they go.'

'So, you see, there really isn't anything standing in our way, is there?'

'Well, if you put it like that then I suppose there isn't,' she said, her hazel eyes sparkling and her heart knocking against her ribcage.

'So if I were to ask you if you have feelings for me, what would your answer be?'

This time Shona really was rendered speechless, but then she reached up and entwined her arms about his neck, and her kiss told him all he needed to know.

The one person who wasn't the slightest bit surprised by the news of their romance was Mrs Tynedale.

'Anyone can see the two of you are made for each other,' she said a couple of days later, as they sat drinking tea on the terrace. She gave a little smile.

'You know Oliver was doing me a great favour when he agreed to buy my shares in the rose nursery and the land, but as for Paddy's Field . . . I really didn't want to sell that, so this morning I rang him up and, as the sale hasn't been finalised yet, I think he might just be persuaded to let me keep it.'

THE END

When Richard employs Annie to update the computer system for his company, she finds herself, through circumstance, living in his house. Although they are attracted to each other, Richard's daughter, Katie, takes a dislike to her. Added to this, Annie suspects that Richard is in love with someone else, so she allows herself to be drawn to Steve, Richard's accountant. Annie feels she must choose between love and a career — how can the complications in her life be resolved . . . ?

ENCHANTED VOYAGE

Mavis Thomas

Lauren was a reluctant member of the family holiday group on a sea cruise, taking in Italy, Greece and Turkey. All her thoughts were of him: she agonised over Grant's accident, his operation, and his forthcoming marriage — to Elaine . . . However, whilst on the *Bella Italia*, Lauren became deeply involved with a charismatic member of the entertainment team . . . and a fellow passenger — a teacher and his two difficult children . . .

WHERE THE BLUEBELLS GROW WILD

Wendy Kremer

Stephen employs Sara, a landscape designer, to improve the appearance of the gardens of Knowles House, his Georgian mansion. He wants to use innovative ideas to generate additional sources of income and is hoping to hire it out for special events — an attractive garden would boost his chances. Lucy, Stephen's childhood friend, lives with her father on the adjoining country estate. Everyone thinks Lucy and Stephen are made for each other — but then along comes Sara . . .

THE BUTTERFLY DANCE

Rosemary A. Smith

It's 1902 and life, for Katherine Johnson, has been rather mundane, living with her Aunt Phoebe and Uncle Zachariah in their house on the coast. However, on her twentieth birthday, she meets Kane O'Brien on the beach and suddenly her thoughts are all of him. But will the circumstances of Kane's birth prevent her Aunt from accepting their love for one another? What is the mystery of the beautiful keepsake box? And where will the butterfly dance lead them?

LONG SHADOWS

Margaret Mounsdon

When Fiona Dalrymple's grand-mother dies, Fiona is shocked to learn that Doreen wasn't actually her grandmother at all . . . Her grandfather's first wife, Ellie Mars-den, is still alive and when Fiona meets her, Ellie has a further shock for Fiona: she also has a brother. What's more, Tim has disappeared and Fiona is charged with the task of finding him . . . so why does Rory, Tim's handsome boss, seems intent on being more of a hindrance than a help?

LEAVING HOME

Cara Cooper

Flora Canning's bags are packed. She's ready to begin a fresh life in New York, leaving her handsome friend Richard Cross devastated at her departure. But plans don't always work out, and a family tragedy forces Flora to stay a while longer. Then fabulously wealthy Nate Campbell enters her life with an offer most women couldn't refuse, and Flora has to learn who to trust and whether it is better to rule with your head or with your heart.